0

DION ANJA

Vertigo Peaks

THE VERTIGO LEGACY
BOOK 1

Content Warnings

Vertigo Peaks contains sensitive material, including but not limited to: anxiety, body horror, blood, consumption of alcohol and drugs (voluntary and involuntary), mentions of domestic abuse (physical and emotional), grief, gore, mention of wounds, misogyny, depiction of murder, sexual content

Book Cover Design by Getcovers

ASIN: B0BWGSQQC2

ISBN: 9786250080795

1st edition 2024

I

SHE WALKED, TORMENTED BY faces. They were all she saw: faces solemn and split with hunger; brows knitted like a surgeon's thread; lips tight as the barren land she trod, grumbling, spitting; and eyes riveted on her—eyes without luster, hard and relentless. Valerie tried to hold her head high as she swept the narrow alleys, arm in arm with her husband.

The fading, brittle joy of autumn had slipped by into the heavy frost of November. The golden leaves were piled, rotting in corners, and Valerie breathed fumes of burnt coal. Soon, the white breath of winter would blanket the peaks with snow, catching the naked trees and surrounding the thatched roofs and chimneys.

She peeked at her husband. He was a slim, short man, and he leaned forward when he walked. Instead of a mouth, he had a thick, black mustache that bristled the hair on the back of Valerie's head. His face was still now, though a ghost of a smile creased his cheeks and somehow, it filled Valerie with dread.

Even though she had not seen many places before, Valerie knew that this town was not a sight to behold. Poverty and famine took over what was once a merchants' hub. Children were pulling on their mothers' skirts with grizzled, moth-eaten sweaters and hats, some even barefoot, crying for a bigger piece of bread. Mothers stroked their unkempt hair, sighed, and turned to meet their colorless faces. Valerie suspected they did not want her husband to feel bereft as they pinched the children's hollow cheeks to bring them color as Valerie and her husband passed them by. She thought of her uncle's cottage, her own calloused hands and swollen legs, exhausted by the day's work, and she felt tired again, unmoored by her sadness. But she recovered quickly when her husband—the infamous Ethan Vertigo—harshly tugged her back.

"Stop staring at them, you'll scare them off. Just smile and wave like I do," he whispered in her ear. "Yes, my dear," she said quietly and turned to her side. His eyes were vacant, and Valerie stumbled on the rough, stony ground when he released her arm. A few giggles and sneers erupted from the crowd, and some shook their heads in protest immediately, punctuating the couple's little trip to make amends.

A few weeks ago, when Valerie had just been married and left her uncle's cottage behind, her marriage felt less like a blessing than a crime against the people she walked amongst now, shoving everything politely hidden behind the hills. She peered back through the crowd and saw, in the lurid glare of the oil lamps, its pointed roof piercing the gray sky like a cathedral's spire—Vertigo Peaks. The manor-house stood tall and proud in the middle of the forest, overlooking the little town and its meandering, gravel road. Yet, its glistening, paned windows and dark, stone walls felt like an imposition, and Valerie had the impression it wasn't right to look at it.

After that lurid night, it was not right at all.

"You tricked us, then you took this harlot to bed, the seed of our misery, of silence, that turned you away from us."

Valerie felt the tension growing inside of her and knew something had to happen soon. A man snatched her arm and spat in her face. "Ethan!" she squeaked. The crowd burst into laughter. They began to gawk at her as if she were the devil incarnate. Before she could run away, another woman, who had broken away from the crowd, appeared by her side with a grin, and dug her nails into her shoulders. Valerie screamed at the sudden pain, trying to push the woman away.

"You turned away from our tradition." She tipped Valerie's chin. Then, raising her voice, she continued, "You fed us to the curse of that damned manor! You wed the perfect resemblance of that poor soul, lost because of you!"

She was flushed, eyes crazed and delirious at having so blatantly endured this insult. Valerie had just taken notice of her polished boots and fine, long dress when Ethan flung her across the crowd and the shouting dwindled. The rush disappeared. The swarming crowd stood still with a ring of sweat on their sullen faces as Ethan danced between her and the woman with his hands in the air.

"Cecilia—Mrs. Harker—please, put a stop to this. I apologize for the inconvenience and grievances we've caused. But my wife is rather exhausted and perplexed by the wedding."

The woman—who Valerie now assumed to be one of her husband's acquaintances—scoffed.

"Do you think this starts and ends with your wedding night, Ethan? Mrs. Vertigo? A bout of plague is upon us because of your family! They found another girl by the docks this morning and it's all because you cannot get your cunt in line. You'll ruin us like you ruined your family!"

People resumed cursing and flailing. She blinked as their crazed laughter filled the air while Mrs. Harker, pulling on her husband's coat, was swinging her long arms at Valerie breathlessly. She was left standing inside a circle of an angry mob, dragging their feet around her, ready to attack, shoulders hunched in anticipation. Valerie did not know what they were talking about. She cast a gloomy look at her husband, who did not take notice of her at all.

Eventually, the doctor was the one who saved them. Valerie remembered his squirmish face from that horrid wedding night. His hands replaced her husband's in a matter of seconds, and every time Valerie tried to squirm away from his touch, his grip tightened.

"Please, Mrs. Vertigo," he said in a raspy voice. "Come with me."

Meanwhile, her husband tried to free himself. "Cecilia, please do not make a scene," he begged. "Let us go."

The words were like blood in water. Ethan Vertigo committed the cardinal sin of pleading. He could be defeated; he could be replaced. In the blink of an eye, the masses surrounded them, and more people flooded the narrow alley than Valerie could see. Their steps echoed on the cobblestones, and she listened to their angry voices which raged around her like a battering ram.

"Call the police immediately!" Ethan yelled in his flight, slowly making his way toward her and the doctor. Her husband's face took on a look of sternness as his eyes were set on the people, bearing the sound of fierce groans and dangerous calls with a contracted brow when the first stone hit his chest.

Then he came, looked up at them and realized they were trapped in the middle of this pandemonium, carried away by the throng of men and women—who had been voiceless and breathless before—like a weed before the wind. The look of defiance disappeared from his face.

Ethan Vertigo was white with fear. Valerie felt her teeth clattering as the two men squeezed her. Retreat was not possible. It became increasingly difficult to draw a breath and her chest started to hurt from all the pressure. Suddenly, her eyes began to well up with tears and her throat felt scorched, as if she had been thrown into fire.

Her mouth formed a "No!" but the deep growl in the sea of people was more dreadful than before. A rock whizzed through the air. She watched its descent in amazement, feeling like a coward still, as it hit her forehead. It drew a veil of light in her vision and blinded her for a moment. She fell on her knees, lying breathless on the cold ground. The dull thump of feet filled the silence in her head. The thread of dark blood trickling down her face kept her dimly conscious as the doctor folded his arms around her.

"Push them away!" he exclaimed. His voice quivered with rage. Then, he gently lifted her off the ground and put her head on his shoulder. "Strike them if you must!"

Her husband's voice called out from a distance. "But they won't stop! They're yelling, they won't draw back!"

"Damn, let them yell!" the doctor shouted. "Make way for us. I'll carry her to my office, and you follow me!"

She cried without restraint when she opened her eyes in the doctor's office. She clung to the door frame to steady herself while her blood dripped on the brass knob. Pain throbbed in her head. Her sobs became uncontrollable, for her mind was quelled by the thought of the unfaltering, spiteful mob lurching toward them, open-eyed and open-mouthed, arms folded and hands holding stones, the trance of their malice too unfathomable to reason with. She did not know how they had moved past their bodies and their terrible anger, but the relief was heavier.

Ethan bore her into the small kitchen while the doctor mixed some liquids in a vial. "You must rest," he said. "And you must clean your apartment," she replied, holding a piece of shredded rag in one hand, before she blushed to her hairline. "I apologize," she quickly added. "I'm quite shaken." But the doctor was unbothered.

"Your senses must have returned then, which is good," he chuckled. "And you're right. I must make an occasion to call for a maid."

Ethan handed her a handkerchief with the steady composure with which he seemed to do everything. The noble, defiant look returned to his face, despite the ongoing turmoil outside. The mob was still mumbling, pounding on their door, and cursing while her husband sat next to her and smiled scornfully. A gleam of certainty had returned to his eyes and Valerie forgot herself for a moment, feeling intrigued by the intensity of his tranquil mood. What was he thinking? Was he in pain as she was, infuriated by the grand failure of their short town visit, and filled with a desire to reproach this marriage?

She shook her head. No, this was not fair. They had a rocky start; their hand was not dealt fairly. They would not be ridden with regret or tormented by the memories of their first night at Vertigo Peaks. Soon, they would be happy, find their footing, and nurture a cozy routine. They would spend the early hours of the morning in bed together, whispering stories about nothing in particular.

Then they would have breakfast in their bright drawing room, with scalding hot tea that would seep through their noses and porridges and bacon and eggs. Then children. Surely, they would have children, who would fill their days with unspeakable joy and mirth. The wedding night did not matter; they could try again.

She jumped when a woman shouted her name and kicked the door. In that fleeting moment, she was captured by her dream, which left a gaping hole in her chest. She did not know which hurt her the most: the wound on her forehead or the aching of her heart? She had no idea she was so empty.

With trembling fingers, she crossed the room and stood in front of the dirty mirror. She wiped the wound clean, panting heavily, and as she caught her face in the mirror, she realized she looked ghastly and wan. Her skin had taken on a grayish, sickly pallor, and her chest heaved up and down forcefully. She looked away, pursing her lips in discomfort.

The doctor handed her the vial and gestured towards the sofa. Valerie followed, unintentionally scanning the cold chamber where the shabby but soft, red carpets, the velvet sofa, and an assortment of chairs filled the room. Several shelves lined the walls—which were otherwise empty—and Valerie saw the dusty medical kits, a variety of tools, and piles of books laying around. His desk was overflowing with scraps of paper and unused ink, and a thick seal of crimson wax protruded amidst the chaos. It was obvious that this was a place reserved solely for work, but Valerie could not help but think of the streak of light slanting on the carpets when she saw the faded line.

She had just sat down on the sofa, gulping the foul-smelling mixture in the vial as fast as she could, and the doctor started bandaging her wound when the door shook on its hinges once more. She jumped to her feet, almost dropping the bottle, and Ethan rushed to peer through one of the windows. He pulled a watch from his pocket with the initials E.V. His eyes darted across the street for a moment. She wondered what he was thinking. She always felt she was barred entrance to his thoughts, only moving in his periphery like a spirit, waiting and listening.

"The police should arrive at any moment," he said. His voice was steady and low, and Valerie would not know the difference unless she saw his flared nostrils and the beads of sweat rolling down his temple. He was angry and perplexed.

"They'll tire themselves out soon enough," said the doctor, sitting on a chair across from her, his hands miraculously tending her wound. Valerie swallowed hard and fidgeted with her wedding ring until he was done. The throbbing was worse, but she let the room spin in a tight web with a surprising amount of resilience. It suddenly became unbearably hot, but she could not move to loosen her collar. Any sudden movement seared her limbs, so she sat motionless and averted her face from the bodice of her dress, which was mottled with blood stains. Instead, she looked at her husband who, twirling the tip of his mustache rather too quickly, stared at the crowd outside.

He straightened his back when the boom of batons rushed through the air and connected with the mob. The blows were incessant; Valerie imagined the police swinging their arms as the cries of the people pierced Valerie's ears, but Ethan turned to her slowly and said, "It's time to go home."

2

A FEW DAYS AFTER the farce of their violent trip in the town, the doctor paid Ethan and Valerie a visit at Vertigo Peaks. It was a crisp, November morning. The grass along the gravel road was withering and frosted, and the white sunlight settled onto the peaks and shone over the branches. Every now and then, a squirrel darted across their yard, mouth full of acorns, dancing up and down the trees, chattering and scurrying through the leaves, and hiding its nuts before it got too cold. Valerie could see the smoke billowing over the rooftops, but the steamed window of their parlor blocked her view of the harbor and the gray stillness of the sea. It almost seemed to blend with the rippled sky, stroking the surface the way an artist's brush would touch the canvas.

Her heart was heavy. She had her cross-stitch to keep her company while her husband bent over his letters on his desk, his finger trailing the edge of the curved letter opener. His countenance was dark and distant, and a grave reflection pervaded his features. One of his eyes winked at intervals, lending an unkind likeness to the portrait above. She perceived the man's rigid long limbs, the same proud arch of his brow, the same dark glare in his eyes. The way Valerie's pulse sped up terrified her. All she saw in the man's features was Ethan Vertigo, so grand and so distinct, and it did not help that he bore the nature of his father, Emery Vertigo, like a proof of his everlasting legacy. The Vertigo Legacy. *My legacy*, Valerie thought.

Then why did Mrs. Harker scream about a curse upon this house, as if something ominous in the waiting drew near? What did she see in her face that called for a lingering, angry look or that vicious attack? Who was this poor soul that was lost because of her husband?

Valerie sighed. She had tried, in vain, to engage him in conversation, but there was no answer. But she needed to know before she could put the matter to rest. She raised her eyes, got up, and walked to her husband's desk as he furiously scrawled on thick sheets of paper. Black ink began to bleed on to the page, but Ethan did not take notice. Valerie did not know what made him scribble this fervently, but the questions pounding her head kept her away from asking. Once the ink was dry, he folded the letter in half and slipped it into an old envelope. He cleaned his stained fingers with cloth before he raised his head, and all the while, she waited expectantly like a child.

"How may I help you?" he asked. His eyebrows were still furrowed with concern and fury, but in the depths of his eyes, something glowed faintly. Valerie cleared her throat and played with her ring, as if the aloof tone of his voice did not offend her. She could walk into a store right now and receive the same treatment or hear the same words from a clerk.

"That day...what was Mrs. Harker talking about?" she inquired. "She did not speak in earnest, did she?"

Her voice faltered and, for a second, she thought she might collapse. Ethan leaned back in his chair and blinked slowly. His silence was becoming painful, though Valerie did not know why.

She asked, "What about the girl...Mrs. Harker said they found another girl on the docks. Who was she?" He continued twirling the letter opener, faster and faster, and his pale face furrowed deeper. His eyes seemed to fix on the wall behind her, staring so intently that Valerie felt herself blushing.

"It was a very tiring day for all of us. I would advise you not to heed Mrs. Harker's words." He gave her a knowing smile that did not quite reach his eyes, then quietly dropped the letter opener. "Don't you fret now, Mrs. Vertigo. Do not be under the illusion that this is your duty as my wife. You shall endure harsher words and tongues will rise against you. However, conversations are nothing more than a frivolous pastime in this town. Love me and honor my house, for this alone will bring you comfort and inspire absolute confidence."

He put his hands on her shoulders, bending his neck to meet her eye. Valerie stood in front of him, motionless, not knowing what to do with his words. She was perplexed, however, as to why her husband spoke so assuredly, when she so vividly remembered Mrs. Harker's wild eyes and that bloodthirsty mob. They were certain their fate was tied by him, walking day and night under a curse of Ethan Vertigo's creation. How could he be so careless and unreserved when she was constantly reminded and tormented by the weight of their accusations and the doubt that followed?

But she became nervous that some turn in the conversation would bring that expression of frustration back to his face again. Thus, she turned aside and hid her face, trying to grow calmer and repeating his words over and over. If she could, she would keep his voice in her head forever. It was an instinct to soothe, to relieve the pressure. Yes, those people were bitter. Why? Because Valerie had refused to partake in their dubious interests on her wedding night. That's why they were running from alley to alley, spreading unspeakable rumors about her and her husband. They were jealous of her being the mistress of Vertigo Peaks, and so they attacked, seeing the breath of life they would never fathom written on her face, as the brutes they were.

"I must make haste. But—ah! My dear friend will take great pleasure in accompanying you. Isn't that right, my friend?"

Ethel—the housekeeper, maid, or cook, Valerie was not sure—entered the room, followed by the doctor. Ethan had already put on his coat and strode out of the parlor when the doctor approached her with a shy smile.

"Yes, sir," he said as he took off his hat and sank into a fancy curtsy. "Good day, madam."

Valerie thought he was glad to see her. She smiled back. A nervous, yet gentle smile. She liked the ease of his manner. Perhaps it was because he was not like her husband. He seemed collected, correct, and cordial.

"Good day, doctor. You must be very cold," she muttered. "Please, have a seat. Would you like a cup of tea?"

He nodded and took a seat near the crackling fire. "Yes, thank you very much."

She threw her cross-stitch aside, hesitating for a moment. Then she rang the bell. The suspense and agony of that pealing sound stirred something inside her. She was not used to ringing bells for tea, giving orders, or approving the menus. She did not know what to say. She could not help it. It was morbid and stifling, and it did not help that she was lacking subtleties and nicety of speech, sitting in a sweat of uncertainty. Valerie had not experienced or observed the niceties of living. It was the first time she had ever encountered such a lavish display, and these things disturbed her. She felt dull at once, her hands on her lap, a set anxiety in her eyes.

They sat for a while in silence. Then the doctor addressed her with deference. "How are you doing on this gloomy morning?"

"I'm quite well, thank you. How fortunate I am to see you in such fine spirits today as well!"

"The pleasure is mine, madam. I do appreciate the rush of frigid air, as it keeps my senses awake." He cleared his throat. Suddenly, his whole face grimaced. She found herself looking at the downward turn of his mouth, heart thumping and anxious. "I must ask you about the unfortunate—"

Ethel returned; her hands flat against the front of her apron. "Yes, ma'am?"

Valerie gave a jump, pushed her seat in sudden panic, and laced her hands against the front of her dress like a servant. At first, she was shocked, and distinctly embarrassed. Her face sank down and she glanced away. Her throat was dry, and she could not swallow. The doctor remained silent, his hands between his knees, and Ethel's mouth was pinched into a tight line. She sensed that they resented her—she felt certain of that. For a moment, annoyance flashed in their faces. This was not what Mrs. Vertigo was intended to do. She sat down abruptly, creaking the seat back into its position. They were waiting for an answer though, much to her dismay.

The color flooded her face. She crushed into humiliation and sizzling shame she had not felt since her uncle once kicked her out of the house.

"Will you bring us the tea tray?" she muttered. Ethel gave a quick nod and scurried away. Her boots clicked on the hardwood floor, out the door, and down the hall.

They drank their tea, for the most part, in silence. Then the doctor spoke slowly, thoughtfully.

"Mrs. Vertigo, that incident was a vile attack on your person. And I'm filled with remorse and regret for having arrived too late. I should not have failed you so gravely."

"Sir, please do not blame yourself. The fault lies not with you. In fact, I ought to apologize. I should have been more vigilant, more aware of the dangers. I should have behaved in a more decorous manner. It does not help that I have a little sense of propriety, grace, and intelligence. It does not help that he does everything naturally, with such poise."

The haste of her passion left her breathless, and she was on the verge of tears. How could she open her heart to a man she barely knew, her husband's best friend? In spite of herself, she raised her eyes, looking straight at him. Patches of blushes came all over her face. The doctor was staring back at her, steady and sharp.

"You must not say that," he said.

"Why? It's true."

"It was neither a failure of decorum nor determination. Mrs. Vertigo, I should say that your husband is a great man. Indeed, he's too gallant and too generous, maybe even more than his father. I consider him kin, my brother. But he is, if I may be so bold, rather imprudent." Valerie's arms hung motionless at her side. He continued, his eyes drooped and his voice a whisper. She felt a quiver of fear.

He looked very agitated. She feared she had upset him, and the realization of this saddened her. She regretted confessing her insecurities to a stranger, and made an attempt to regain her composure. A soft smile lingered on her lips. "Let us not dwell on the past anymore. Instead, let us focus on the present and ensure that—"

Yet, the doctor was fervent with his beliefs. His shallow breaths clouded his look; it was the only motion visible on his body. His head was thrown a little back, the loss of the spark in his eyes making his firmness more evident. She had detected the heavy shadow of his dark hair. She was startled, most of all, by the latent fervor, which unfolded under his calloused, trembling hands like a torrid, hasty storm. "Our paths are veiled with shadows, madam. They leave marks upon our characters, but we must learn to walk with them."

He occupied himself with the saucer for half a minute or so, offering his silence as an expression of gratitude, then stood up abruptly. She did not speak. She did not move. She wondered whether he knew why Mrs. Harker taunted them. Was he another actor in the town's schemes? Or was it all a discreet and amiable gesture? She would never dare ask, of course. She caught one more glance at his face before he left the room.

3

SOMETHING WAS WRONG. VALERIE could not put her finger on it, but a harrowing sense seeped into her brain. Maybe it was the gust of frigid wind whistling down the manor's chimneys and slapping her cheeks, or the orange light of guttering candles in the distance. The air around her looked strange, like it was filled with ash. The smell of grease smoke and soot hung low and dense, which blotted out the entire town from view.

She dragged the heel of her palm over her nose and made towards the drawing room, silently closing the door behind her. Nothing stirred. She was alone. Meanwhile, the moon shone bright, dancing silver and serene on her face, casting a gentle glow upon her stiff features. The snow was fast approaching. Her fingers toyed with the emerald green stone of her ring, while her mind wandered, a sense of unease lingering in the air. She thought of all the things Ethan and the doctor had said and how much easier it would be if she knew the truth. If her husband, as Mrs. Harker and all the livid townspeople had made him out to be, was at the mercy of a curse, why did he marry her and drag her into this? If

19

that was the case, didn't she have a right to know the truth? To demand answers?

Valerie's head was spinning. No, that wasn't fair. If it weren't for the doctor and her husband, she wouldn't have escaped the wrath of the crowd that day. She saw herself, gasping for breath and a pang of terror going through her chest, and the frozen look on her attackers' faces, stricken down by despair and white-hot anger. With gnarled and bony hands, they had hooked their accusations onto her and Ethan. They were vile, ungrateful traitors, loyal only to themselves. In spite of his charity, they had attacked her husband. No, she should not take heed of their abomination, or wail at the sight of them, for their betrayal was a whisper in the breeze. Always changing, ever shifting with the weight of their corruption. She should ensure they did proper penance and forgive this lapse. She was the mistress of Vertigo Peaks. If there's only one person who could do it, it was her. Then there would be tears no more. Only happiness.

As she sat there, growing weary of contemplating, a nagging pain in the small of her back, Valerie noticed the muted voices drifting in from the adjoining study. Curiosity piqued, she rose from her seat and approached the door. It stood ajar, and through the crack, Valerie could make out a dark figure—the silhouette of her husband. He did not suspect she was in the drawing room. He did not even bother to close the door.

As she approached, the voices became clearer, revealing familiar tones. One belonged to Ethan, low and urgent, while the other was too hushed to distinguish. Valerie's heart skipped a beat. Who was this man? What were they discussing so clandestinely?

With caution, she pressed her ear against the door and strained to catch their words. The first few fragments were indecipherable, mere murmurs of hurried conversation. But then, a sentence floated through the air, catching Valerie's attention and freezing her in place.

"They must cheer for me," Ethan was saying. "I need them to welcome me with open arms when I next visit the town." His voice came through, tinged with desperation and a hunger for validation, which troubled Valerie deeply. "I need the townspeople to truly believe I am still a man of influence and importance."

The study was dimly lit by candles attached to each shelf so that it only made books visible. The thick smoke of cigars and the musty scent of books watered her eyes, but Valerie did not move. There, huddled by the desk, stood the taller figure. She noticed the body stiffen as her husband's words sank in. *If only he would move closer to the light*, she thought. His face was buried too deep in the shadows.

"And how do you propose we achieve such a feat?" the tall figure whispered. Her husband regarded the other man with a sly expression.

"You know, my dear friend, that you hold a certain position in our little town. As the local physician, your words carry weight. I need you to use that influence to ensure that the people cheer for me when I make my grand entrance."

"Bribery, Ethan? Is that the path you wish to take?"

The man came out, rather defiantly, and Valerie saw the doctor's face, his trembling lip, and the set of his jaw clenched.

"Yes, bribery, if necessary," replied her husband. "A few coins to help them forget their inhuman animosity and instead focus on what I brought to this town, the hardships I endured on their behalf, the calamities weighed upon me for their sake. So it is not too unreasonable of me to ask their loyalty, is it, doctor?"

Ethan did not take notice of his friend's silence. He continued, quivering with excitement. His eyes fixed on the ceiling in anticipation, as if waiting for a sign of approval. "Doctor, I trust you can discreetly organize this. Ensure the people are properly compensated. I want this done before my next visit. Before I take Mrs. Vertigo to town again."

The doctor jerked his head.

"Mr. Vertigo—" he began, but Ethan silenced him, raising his hand. "My friend, if you are not fit for the task, I can find another man. But Mr. and Mrs. Harker, especially Mrs. Harker, taking control of our town puts you at the end of the rope as well. It saddens me if you so quickly forget the times I helped you ."

Ethan touched his bushy mustache as if to curl it, a defying gesture of warning, Valerie thought, and the doctor became animated.
His face wrinkled and distorted with lines too terrible to behold.
He wiped his brow; his fingers were slick with perspiration. He
nodded reluctantly.

"As you wish, Mr. Vertigo. But remember, the consequences
could be dire if word of this arrangement gets out."

"Oh, doctor, my good friend, I trust you will take every precau-
tion. No one will ever know of our little secret," replied Ethan,
grinning.

Valerie's eyes widened in shock, her hand instinctively flying to
her mouth to muffle her gasp. Her heart was pounding in her chest,
her mind reeling. She was unaware of the extent of her husband's
desperation. He was willing to sacrifice integrity for the fleeting
admiration of the townsfolk. The man she had married, the man
she had believed to be noble and principled, was slipping away
before her very eyes. She replayed their words over and over again,
unable to fathom the motive behind such an elaborate scheme.

The weight of the moment pressed upon Valerie's shoulders.
She knew she couldn't confront Ethan directly—not yet. There
were too many emotions coursing through her, and too many
questions left unanswered. But she also knew that their marriage
would never be the same again.

4

As the horse-drawn carriage made its way down the cobblestone streets of the town, Valerie's heart fluttered with a mix of anticipation and trepidation. She observed the townspeople going about their daily lives, unaware of the sinister scheme that hung over their heads. Beside her, Ethan sat tall and proud, his hazel eyes filled with determination. The muscles on the sides of his head bulged. She had watched him write countless letters, locking himself in his study to find new ways to repair his relationship with the townspeople, planning the details of this trip meticulously.

He was completely oblivious to her knowledge. The deceit she had discovered gnawed at her soul, yet she found herself torn between loyalty and self-preservation.

Valerie was unsure of what awaited them. It had been over a week since the horrifying incident that had befallen them, but she was still very weak. Her body trembled and she broke into a sweat whenever she tried to sleep, seeing the vicious faces of townspeople wavering before her, thin and gaunt, the hard edges protruding beneath their skin.

She brushed a lock of auburn hair away from her face. Her heart was racing as they entered the bustling town square. She saw the doctor first, waiting by a bakery. He cast a long, grim look at their carriage, as if disappointed and in need of an excuse to not be there. It seemed to her that he also had not been sleeping well. He had circles beneath his eyes and his mouth twisted in a frown of disdain. His arms hung motionless at his side, his hands curled into fists, and his shoulders drooped. Something inside her coiled at his expression, like a snake undulating at her feet, then she looked away.

To her dismay, it was the doctor who welcomed them first. He appeared as soon as their carriage came to a halt, holding out his hand so she could get off the carriage. She sat motionless for a moment, her gloved hands clutching onto the edges of her dress. She hesitated, her hand suspended in mid-air, then placed her hand in his. His complexion almost seemed ghastly against the gloomy overcast afternoon and his gaze held a penetrating intensity, as if he knew what she was thinking. A shiver ran down her spine, but she did not falter. His eyes softened for a moment, erasing the unsettling expression. He said, "Fear not, Mrs. Vertigo, my purpose today is to heal, not to haunt."

With a steadying breath, Valerie allowed him to guide her out of the carriage. As soon as her feet touched the ground, she noticed an eerie silence hanging in the air. Shop windows were barred shut, their once inviting displays hidden from view. The scent of freshly baked bread and the melodic tunes of a nearby pub were conspicuously absent. Ethan, sensing her unease, gently squeezed her hand. Valerie noticed a cluster of people, eyes filled with discontent and suspicion, wearing a solemn expression, on either side of the street passing them by. Valerie followed their gaze toward the horizon and saw a line of stern-faced police officers, weighing their batons, ready to quash any sign of disturbance.

With hesitant steps, she followed Ethan. He did not pay attention to the silent protest or the palpable tension hovering about him while the tinkling sound of their contempt did little to quench Valerie's fright. Not a word spilled from their hungry mouths, yet Valerie heard their voices in her restless mind. They resented her; they would always resent her.

"What are you doing?"

She almost choked on her words, hoping the inconspicuous question would put some sense into him. Instead, he waved to the crowd, flashing wide grins and looking straight at their faces. She felt like she was there and not there, cringing at his touch on her arm. "Wave, my dear," he instructed, not breaking his grin. She hesitated, awfully conscious of people's growing animosity, then waved to the crowd reluctantly.

She would go through every motion of his, subject herself to humiliation and calamity, so long as she knew she was safe. All the lies could be forgotten, time would heal all. Her worries belonged to the past. She was Mrs. Vertigo, walking arm in arm with Ethan

Vertigo, shrouded in his everlasting legacy. She would not return to those days when she begged her uncle to spare her a room, give her a moment's break. She would pace the halls of Vertigo Peaks as she wished. She shall ask no more, she would receive.

Her uncle was not a terrible man despite his curt and aggressive hardness and grating voice. He honored his dying brother's wish and took Valerie under his roof after all. Nevertheless, she could not help but feel he resented her too. She always thought her existence must have felt like responsibility to him, who bore its weight grunting and irritated, then he made her pay for it. She always remembered her days at his cottage behind a film of sawdust and tall weeds, scraping the floors until her hands grew rough and calloused, the tips of her fingers as yellow as vinegar, the threat of losing her shelter always imminent.

As they strolled through the sparse thoroughfare, Valerie caught sight of Mrs. Harker perched on the edge of a bench with a group of friends. There was a small, sneering smile on her face, as though she was both amused and annoyed by her, as she turned to meet her eye. For the first time, she noticed her face: it was extremely pale and covered with freckles, her sand covered hair framed her face rather strangely, for it reminded Valerie of balloons. Her little mouth had contorted in a childish frown, making her lips even thinner. She placed a finger on her pursed lips when she noticed Valerie, her face red in the dim light, before Ethan led them down a narrow alley.

The doctor approached them cautiously, placing a hand on her husband's shoulder and whispering in his ear before disappearing from their view. Waves of cheer and applause greeted them. The townspeople, young and old, stood on tiptoes, craning their necks to catch a glimpse of Mr. and Mrs. Vertigo. The residents, adorned in their finest attire, lined the alley, their faces painted with warm enthusiasm. Flowers and ribbons adorned everywhere, as though their arrival was a festive scene. Children, their eyes shining with admiration, skipped alongside them, clutching flowers and offering them as tokens of love.

Valerie's eyes widened as they locked onto the crowd. A young girl approached them and handed her a delicate bouquet of for-get-me-nots. The men lined in front of Ethan, offering him firm handshakes.

"Welcome, sir! Welcome, madam!" cried a man as he broke away from the crowd and approached them. "We have longed for this day, to right the wrongs committed against you. Please, embrace the love and respect we have for you."

"We were blinded by fear that evening," another woman whispered. "But now, we see the error of our ways. Please, forgive us."

She became dizzy with the sea of smiling faces and outstretched hands. She knew this was a fabricated gratitude, one forged with bribery and deceit, as her husband handed out fuzzy clothes and hot meals to people. He had really thought every detail, she thought, surprised to see those who had left the town square, those faces etched with lines of sorrow and frustration, return with interest.

"Spare us some food, Mr. Vertigo!" One yelled. "My boy needs a new coat, my lady!" The other followed. They were surrounded, this time by a throng of destitute yet hopeful people, screaming their names and marching in blissful awe. Valerie liked the passion with which they chanted her name, echoing in waves of assurance and honor, no matter how fabricated it was. Maybe her husband had indeed whispered the truth: it was best for them to hold the keys of the town.

"Ah, Lady Vertigo, what a pleasant surprise!" Mrs. Harker remarked, her voice dripping with false delight. Valerie turned around and saw Mrs. Harker and her cohort, pushing the crowd hurriedly, strained smiles on their lips.

Valerie curtsied in response. "Mrs. Harker, the pleasure is all mine."

Ethan inclined his head towards the group with a reserved smile. His eyes glinted as he spoke. "My lady, I trust you are well on this fine day?"

"Indeed, I am quite well, thank you," Cecilia Harker replied, casting a lingering gaze at him. Their tailored gowns and the scent of freshly cut roses wafted up to her, exuding a commanding presence that Valerie found to be threatening. Her fingers were laden with jewels.

"Might I extend an invitation to you for a dinner party at my humble house next week? It would be a pleasure to host such esteemed guests."

Valerie's eyes narrowed ever so slightly, recognizing the subtle challenge hidden within Mrs. Harker's words. She looked over at her husband, as if she was intruding on him. His expression changed from surprise to triumph, his eyes declaring that he was familiar with Cecilia Harker's game. The stage was his, and the rules were clear: he would emerge victorious. Nevertheless, he maintained his polite facade. "How kind of you, Lady Harker. We shall be honored to accept your invitation."

Mrs. Harker's lips curled in a sagging smile, so Valerie could see the gap between her front teeth. They bid each other farewell, promising to meet again at their appointed time. The townspeople were still at their heels when the doctor approached them. He looked almost relaxed, not like an animal in a cage, anxiously waiting to see what might happen next. He stood tall again, unclenching his fists. Valerie chose her moment carefully, unable to withstand this burden any longer, and stood with him before their carriage arrived.

"I know what you're doing," she said, trembling all over, as hot tears of shame pricked her eyes. "I overheard your conversation with my husband."

5

VALERIE GLIDED THROUGH THE long halls of Vertigo Peaks with an air of terrible weakness. The once opulent walls, adorned with intricate tapestries and gilded frames, now displayed a haunting sight, for Valerie saw the wallpapers, once vibrant and alive with color, now peeling and faded, revealing the ravages of time. Her heart sank as she traced her fingers along the peeling edges, her touch causing flakes of paint to dislodge and cascade to the worn wooden floor below. For all its imposing structure, Vertigo Peaks was as delicate as a sick child.

She couldn't help but feel a deep sense of sorrow, for she had believed the manor-house to be her sanctuary, her refuge from the outside world. It was not true. Even the very walls were succumbing to decay and neglect, the ground beneath her grumbling. A low, ominous sound echoing through the halls, as if protesting against the weight of the people it had housed for centuries.

Valerie's steps faltered and she clutched at the banister, worn smooth by the hands of generations past. The place was unnerving. Slowly she became conscious of her shivering, the sound of creaking floorboards beating against her chest like ghastly whispers, settling upon Vertigo Peaks like a thick veil.

"What is this place?" she asked herself as she ascended a grand staircase, finding it hard to believe that this was indeed her home. She had not seen this wing before. It was as if it weren't part of Vertigo Peaks. The chandeliers, once ablaze with sparkling crystals, now hung in mournful silence, their flickering candles long extinguished. The musty scent of decay filled the air, mingling with the scent of dried flowers and fading memories. The same sense of old-fashioned grandeur, frail beauty that covered the house was eerily missing from these walls. A strong smell of dampness and rot, reminiscent of dungeons, pervaded its dark halls. The candle in her hand cast long shadows on the walls as the dust-covered portraits stared down at her with hollow eyes, their subjects long departed from the mortal world. She paused and gazed upon one in particular. With trembling hands, she brushed away the thick layer of dust that had settled on it.

It was as though she was looking at some distant, dulled version of herself, marred by time. The oil portrait was framed in ornate gold, lingering at the inevitable edge of decay, a wistful reminder of the Vertigo legacy. It was her exact likeness. Valerie saw her own long nose, the arched brow, the same auburn hair hanging in ringlets, even the creases under the eyes, all mirrored in this young woman. A sense of unease washed over her. It was uncanny. The only difference was her long sighs echoing in the empty halls.

How could this be? She turned away from the portrait in disgust and terror, weighed down by her thoughts. It must have been a mistake; she had not sat for a portrait in her entire life. Could her husband indeed have been hiding something from her?

Valerie's mind wandered back to that forsaken day—Mrs. Harker's gloved hands on her chin, her eyes as green and riveting as a willow. The lost soul, the unmistakable resemblance. Was Cecilia Harker talking about the lady in the portrait?

A knock at the door jolted Valerie from her thoughts. Startled, she turned to find Ethel standing at the threshold, her face etched with concern and fear. "Madam," she said, her voice filled with genuine worry. "Are you alright? You look rather pale."

Valerie sensed the tension in her voice as Ethel's gaze flickered to the portrait, and a sense of disquiet passed over her face. "Ethel," Valerie replied, pointing to the portrait, her voice laced with apprehension. "Who is this woman?"

For a moment, the room was still, as if holding its breath. Valerie faced the young woman, suddenly agitated and angry, waiting for an answer. She felt the heat rising up to her cheeks and her mouth was so dry that she could not swallow. The maid—or the housekeeper, Valerie was not quite sure still—fumbled nervously with her cap.

"It's...Mr. Vertigo's sister, madam."

"How odd it is that we haven't been introduced! Where is she?" Valerie said, feeling the steady pressure of her nails digging into her skin. She straightened up with determination and clenched her jaw.

She knew the answer before Ethel opened her mouth, and she dreaded the moment. Yet, here she was. She should never be the same again, never look the same at her husband or pace the halls of Vertigo Peaks without feeling a sense of imminent threat lurking nearby. She felt a distance so insurmountable, deep within her bones, that her heart ached with yearning. In the face of loss, she wished she could return to her old days when none of this mattered.

Ethel averted her eyes when she spoke, staring down at her feet. "She sadly passed away a year ago, madam."

Valerie sat at the parlor, sipping her third cup of tea, eyes misty and unseeing with the same languor that she had as she entered Vertigo Peaks for the first time. It was a warm afternoon when she got married, the pleasant clear sky and hot sun dancing on her skin, the wild poppies dancing in the breeze, yet she had moved as if defeated, embarrassingly aware of her rough, rustic edges. It did not make sense then why a lord would want to marry someone like her. Her braids were undone by the time the ceremony was over, the hems of her wedding gown exuded odors of wet grass and wheat. She remembered feeling ashamed of ruining her appearance and no garment would disguise her plainness.

She would have spoken with mellow and slow words perhaps, without the peasant hesitancy; but the sudden, horrifying descent of their wedding night had washed all her reason away. Her cheeks turned cold and colorless as she stepped into the room. A wave of sudden heat, the musky smell of velvet curtains curling on the floor, she tucked behind the crook of her husband's elbow. When her eyes adjusted to the dimness, she saw the long line of guests, waiting for them, with their hands clasped as if in prayer, held together by a string of murmurs.

"They're here for us. They will prepare us for...tonight," Ethan said, his cheeks flushed. It was a whirl of glow that Valerie had never seen before on his face. "Our marriage is sacred. This town has been waiting for this forever."

"I beg your pardon?" Valerie asked, out of breath and unblinking, as though she was a rabbit caught in a hunter's light. The room suddenly felt oppressive and stifling. No one heard her faint sigh as all eyes were on her husband, who stepped back, astonished by the resentment in her voice.

"Tonight," he said, emphasizing every word. "They will stay with us and pray for an heir." She watched as his hazel irises shrank, staring at her with a stern and relentless expression. Valerie lowered her gaze. Her heart was pounding in her throat.

If she were to say a word, would he walk away and call the marriage off? Would he send her back to her uncle's cottage, where she was not welcome anymore with nothing but a tarnished name to carry until the end of her days? Valerie tightened her grip on her husband's arm and forced a smile.

She remembered the young girl who helped her get ready. Kind eyes and a timid smile that framed her sullen face, her quick breaths stroking Valerie's cheeks. She was awed by her duty—serving Mrs. Vertigo on her wedding night—as she coiled Valerie's hair into a tight bun. Older women were preparing the bath, filling the tub with liquids. White froth turned into gray waves; smoke of incense rose like vine. Her spine relaxed as though she ran through a stream, tracing the lightness of her body in sweet ripples. She dreamed of herself in forms unimagined. She couldn't think of anything better as the room melted before her eyes.

"You shall cherish and love him. Make him your horizon, and grace you shall receive. Confide in him and give him a child," they cried out with a hissing breath. At once Ethan grabbed her by the arm before they could wrap her in towels, and drew her to bed.

She caught sight of the large group as Ethan pulled the sheets, the physician among them. The room was overflowing with people, holding hands, singing a supple tone, and watching as Ethan leaned over her. Beads of sweat rolled from his chin to her bare chest. She couldn't breathe.

"Get them out!" She emitted a long, hoarse shriek. Her uncle had told her a wedding night could never be fully known, in unsatisfying and inevitable ways, and she realized she was foolish to expect privacy. She turned her head in disgust, trying to cover her exposed thighs and chest.

"They will watch us and see the marriage consummated," he breathed down her neck. "It's tradition." She wriggled under him as a worm might in the mud. It was not a tradition, but perversion and voyeurism, she thought as his hand climbed up her thigh, his sweaty chest against hers. Her gaze jumped between the myriad of people—the timid girl, the doctor, the women who bathed her—and the ceiling. Her fists were full with the crumpled sheets, and she laid still until the roar of people calmed a little, scathing tears making a path to her ears.

She usually weaved her movements slowly, without haste or much deliberation, encompassing nothing beyond her senses; a shiny slate of unprovoked thoughts and free flowing emotions. Yet, when people lurched toward their bed to snatch the blood-soaked sheet and wave it like a flag, she sprung to her feet and screeched like a hell-bound creature, not caring about the flush of her cheeks or the aching between her legs.

"Get out," she screamed. "Stop it!"

She felt cumbered and nauseous. They swooned over their bed, chanting the same two words over and over again—Save us! Save us! Save us!—rubbing the silk against their teary eyes and wet cheeks where her thick, coppery blood began to dry already. She ripped it away from their brute hands and tossed it into the fire as they grumbled and stomped their feet. Some said, "Leave it be!" while others cried, "You'll ruin us!"

"It's tradition," her husband kept saying, barely moving his lips. Valerie curled on the bed, breathless and trembling in fear, as dust fell from the ceiling, her back vibrating as if the house sighed in relief. What did she think would happen marrying a man of importance? She would adorn herself with rings and live content forevermore? She was a fool. Of course people would expect charity and attention. Of course they would demand reverence for orders and traditions and decorum.

She sat upright with a start when she heard Ethel, startled by the blur of her curtsy. Her hands were trembling. "You summoned me, my lady?"

"Have a seat, please."

Ethel turned around, thinking Valerie was talking to someone else, and blushed when she realized she was being addressed. "I am afraid I cannot do that, Mrs. Vertigo."

Valerie raised a brow. "Why?" Ethel started biting her lower lip, her gaze fixed on the red carpet. "I am your maid, madam. I cannot."

This time it was Valerie who blushed. But she gathered herself quickly and took on a somewhat firm tone. She needed answers and embarrassing her maid would not help get them. "Why is that wing of the house so neglected?" she asked, swallowing hard. If she had been more experienced and educated, she might find a way to frame her questions with quick wit. But she was just a naive peasant who had married a noble man, so all her ways had to be blunt.

Ethel twitched the folds of her apron. She searched the room and spoke quickly like a prisoner who had taken a plea bargain. "Mr. Vertigo's father was accustomed to that wing when he was alive. After his demise, his sister moved her chambers there. But...Her tragic death was enough for Mr. Vertigo to abandon that wing entirely."

A mix of shock and disbelief coursed through Valerie's veins. Why hasn't Ethan mentioned her once before? Why did he keep such a secret? Why did everyone know this sister and her lost soul but her? Her heart was torn between anger and sadness. She had married into a web of deceit, a man who had kept his own flesh and blood hidden away like some shameful secret.

"Why have you concealed her from me then?" She was losing her control, her voice tinged with desperation. She felt the desperate loneliness creeping up on her, the uninterrupted isolation and bleak silence. Her eyes were so full of tears that she couldn't see straight. "Why haven't you uttered a single word?"

The maid's hands trembled more violently, her voice barely above a whisper. "I beg your forgiveness, my lady, but I swear it on my soul that I thought Mr. Vertigo mentioned her to you. He was so fond of her before—"

"What?"

Ethel's eyes darted to the painting hung above the fireplace. Valerie followed her gaze and there was her husband, young and fierce, sitting on a chair. His mother was sitting right next to him, a wistful smile illuminating her countenance, and his father's wrist hung over his shoulder like an iron hand, his imposing stature not less frightening. Befitting for a house like this, she thought.

The maid looked up, meeting Valerie's gaze. "There are whispers amongst the staff and in the town." She hesitated for a moment. "There are those who claim she met her end in a most peculiar way, they say."

Valerie held her breath and clenched her hands together until her knuckles turned white. Outside snow had begun to swirl round the peaks, drifting down in silence. The manor-house was perfectly quiet for once, the only sound coming from the embers of the log fire.

"But they never found the body, madam."

6

THE VOICE HAD BEEN beating outside her heart for hours when one night she woke up with a start. She heard it call her name, yet she sensed it wanted her blood. Its callous cadence didn't let Valerie drowse peacefully. She tossed in her bed like mist on crushed leaves.

"Keep looking at me Valerie," the voice called out, "I'm near. Come closer."

And in that moment, all she knew was her name, splashed in scarlet letters, followed by eyes in deeper crimson shade. The uncertainty of her frenzy and the restlessness disappeared. She was not frightened, for she found a quietly composed, sanguine face looking at herself from the side of her bed. It was a young lady, pretty and curious-looking, kneeling in front of her. Valerie's chest suddenly rose and fell with mirth; she listened with rapture.

"Valerie, come near."

She looked at the lady with calm composure as she caressed her, the delicate touch of her hand made Valerie shiver. Suddenly, the door flung open and she met the thrill of night, drawing towards the lady as a lover made their way to reverie. Its toil, its embrace, its mysticism, like a desperate kiss. That's how she searched for her. Through an act of desperation, movements of sweet dependence upon recognition. To be wanted, to be needed in the exact bones she took shape.

The voice kept calling and she bent like a twig, barely conscious of her bare feet. Her nightgown was billowing up around her ankles; the auburn strands of hair curled up by the wind, brushing her cheeks. Her face quickly became wet from the snow as it cut her cheeks, yet Valerie marched on, treading the earth as lightly as she could for a quick release.

Her throat burned with thirst, her lips parched, tantalized by a breath of bewildering glimpses. Deep in the lush woods, beyond the reach of moonlit hills and wavering cries of owls, lurked a shadow. The intent was clear from the moment she laid eyes upon her crooked figure: to hunt, to gnaw, and satiate its feral ache.

"My dear," it whispered and shot up.

The lady's face appeared again, it was cracked and sunken in places, gleaming in the dark. The white of her eyes were consumed; only a red spark lingered, but it still lit up her entire face and her drooping smile. She was reaching out, pale as the waning moon, but the limbs seemed as though they were cut off. The hue of them was sleek, dark and exuded a certain kind of warmth. Blood trailed through the folds of her dress like a river, sweeping up the weeds and moss.

She moved and Valerie moved.

Famished into surrender, she let her creep closer. Her mouth sparked ominously. Valerie's heart was beating against her chest like a drum. She gasped when the woman tipped her face back. Her back against a tree, she parted her lips to speak but could only give a little whimper.

She leaned in and gave her a kiss. First it was fleeting and glassy like a drizzle against the tall windows in her room; then, it was passionate and devotional like a song.

Soon they became entangled. The woman put her nose against her neck, breathing heavily, and Valerie wondered if she caught on fire. Her limbs seared with pain, where the lady's mouth touched made her burn as blood slipped under her tongue. A tenacious warning. Yet she was soothed by the sensation.

The coppery taste made her wince, but she was too weak to separate herself from the woman. She was reminded of something—a fragment of midnight, words whispered in the dark that she did not want to think about anymore. Lately, her life had been morphing into resentment and aversion, crumbling around her like a broken promise. But this wanting, iridescent and direct, caught herself in between abundance and wanting more. It was her right to hold on to its wings, soar above the frozen wild poppies and leave the dry moors behind.

She ran her hand through the woman's windswept hair and pressed her lips on hers again, slipping under the edge of her world and making a slit in the center. It wouldn't dare to hold and she wouldn't step back.

The woman pushed Valerie's hair back and clawed at her throat until Valerie yelped at the sight of her blood. It wasn't enough. She sank her teeth deep and the skin opened, as if two needles pierced her breast, but Valerie was still dreaming about the poppies. It was strange, having a self to protect and untether from the overgrown roots. But in the woods, her head thrown back and inviting this hungry woman deeper, she was at peace.

The woman drained her blood and she moaned with equal pain and pleasure. Her hands wandered up Valerie's waist then and slipped under her nightgown, circling around her collarbones as though casting a spell. A numbing sensation overtook the pain and ran through her veins.

It devastated her when she pulled back, the back of her throat ached with an unfamiliar blaze, and she wrapped her arms around herself to keep the lady's warmth, the indentation of her body a little longer.

"I won't hurt you," she said. Her voice was hoarse against her ear and she was quiet again for a minute, but then she closed the distance between them and kissed her again, summoning all kinds of thoughts. Dangerous ones, luscious ones.

Valerie rekindled at once and parted her lips, half-awake and in anticipation, as the woman settled between her legs. The salt and blood on the woman's lips mixed with her own blood and the sweet evening tea. Their bodies crashed and the wind whirled around them, reducing everything into a haze, and the woman's loose golden hair whipped against her face.

An earthy smell filled her lungs and she smiled with the realization of this new awakening. What stood in front of her was barely a reflection, rather she took the woman as an omen, ravenous as she was, and a part of her soul. It was alarming and it was beautiful.

A cry ripped through the hush of the woods and the lady startled back, her eyes still fixed on Valerie, then pulled her up to her feet.

"Hey, what are you doing here?" A boy emerged behind the trees, through the hollow. The yellow light of his lantern revealed a long, slender neck. His beard was short and scruffy in a way that gave him a look of prematurity. He began to move swiftly among a grove of bushes, stopping every now and then to jump over thorns, the dry leaves crackling under his feet. "Are you deaf? I'm talking to you!"

Valerie pursed her lips, swaying on her feet as if in a trance, enveloped still in a warm, bright desire. The boy put his hand in the pocket of his long, shabby coat and pulled out something. Valerie could not see it at first then he turned it between his fingers. A handle of a knife. It glistened under the glow of the lantern as he hurried in their direction, leaping over branches and snow.

It was so sudden, and so unlike anything that she had ever witnessed, that Valerie could not even make a sound. The boy's lantern slipped from his fingers and rolled on the ground as the young lady climbed on top of him, pinning his lean body with ease. She buried her face in the boy's neck, like she did to Valerie, while he tried to wriggle from her grasp. He let out a scream, grabbing his throat as fresh blood gushed out, bubbling with foam, blanketing the frozen ground in a small pool of crimson. In his struggle, his eyes found Valerie then widened in shock. His blood-soaked hand extended in her direction, knowing and accusatory.

Valerie slowly became conscious of her surroundings—the austere simplicity of blood sprayed on the deep snow, the very air churning in a sickly odor, the cast of woman's shadow standing over the convulsing boy's bitten neck, the whistles of owls hovering over her head. She tried to keep her head still as she backed away, afraid of making a sudden movement. The woman was not distracted from her work, stiff and panting, so she ran until the rusty gates of Vertigo Peaks rose in front of her, its ornate letters arching high above, catching the silver light of the moon, the punctures on her throat pulsating.

7

THE MORNING WAS VIOLENT. Valerie woke up with a terrible headache, a glossy fog over her brain, and a burning in the back of her throat. When only a dull soreness like a bruise remained, she sat up in the empty bed—she could hear the muffled voices coming through her husband's study—and saw how bleak the day was. The snowfall obscured the peaks from view and made the empty fields indistinguishable from the forest that surrounded them. The wind sang its soft and thrilling tune, the flakes falling slowly, yet for Valerie the day had already faded, hushed and heavy. The hazy impression of the previous night was nothing more than a fickle thought.

Today, she was changed. She could never go back to those early days of timid anticipation and eager hopes, filled with unfamiliar desire and optimism, the likes of which Valerie only remembered from her childhood when she held no responsibilities and played as she wished with the children who lived next door. The cracked mirror above the basin showed her to herself—an old, weary face and the infinitesimal remnant of what she could have been. Her wound healed perfectly, the bulge had disappeared and the cut left a faint violet line on her forehead. Yet Valerie could still feel the dripping blood, the scratching fabric of her bandage when her eyes wandered to the spot the rock hit.

If she married a man of importance, she had thought once, she would be saved from her uncle's wrath. But a husband's hand was no different from the hands of an uncle. They were the same brute, hands still on her throat, despite love. She had fancifully believed love sheltered her, belonged to her. Yet, twisting and turning in front of the cracked mirror, Valerie was struggling to find, from inside her skin, a way out, and maybe be known.

"Why aren't you dressed? Has not Ethel told you?"

The heavy door cracked open, Ethan was standing in the doorway, his eyes ablaze. He closed the distance between them and ran his palms over Valerie's cheeks. She could feel the dampness of his skin against hers, cold and confining, wincing as his fingers ran over the throbbing puncture marks. She buried her chin in the high collar of her nightgown, hoping he did not notice the swell and heat of her scarlet skin. Glancing at the mirror, she noticed a splatter of dark blood and covered the spot with her matted hair in haste.

"What?" replied she, with what she hoped was a steady voice. He shot a worried glance at her, taking in a deep breath, then spoke so slowly it seemed like every word was vital to his existence.

"Mr. and Mrs. Harker expect us this evening for dinner! I suppose the success of our trip urged them to offer an olive branch—but think, dear! All the disturbances we've had, our standing in the society, my reputation...We can secure our future, darling."

Her mind was far away, the memory of his clandestine arrangement with the doctor was still boiling in her stomach. She did not understand the reason behind his obsession with his standing or name; he was already a respectable, rich man, but she still managed to smile.

"I am most delighted," she said, trying to arrange her facial features into a calm expression. Instead, she wanted to say, "I don't understand you. I am horrified by your illicit ways. What secrets lie behind your facade? Why don't you want me the way you want the favorable opinion of this forsaken town?"

He leaned over close, his slender neck bending like a reptile, and planted a kiss between her knuckles, beaming like a schoolboy. "They most kindly will send their carriage. Ours is not sturdy enough for this weather—" He looked out the window, a furrow of anxiety appearing on his forehead, but the spark in his greedy eyes quickly returned before he left the room without another glance at Valerie.

The horse-drawn carriage came to a sharp halt in front of the ivory manor's drive. The click-clack of hooves against cobblestone echoed through the silent road, announcing their arrival. Valerie was sitting beside her husband. The lanterns were already lit, casting a warm, orange glow over his face, disfiguring his features into grimacing, sharp shadows. He had a gleam in his eyes that Valerie could not decide whether malicious or mischievous. Her gloved hands clutched onto the folds of her blue-laced dress. Its ruffled neckline was high, and the sleeves were long enough to cover the bruises thankfully. After Ethan left her room, she inspected herself like a detective, searching for minute details of hurt. She found herself not in a bad shape: a couple scratches from the bushes, splinters in the back of her leg, blooming bruises on her wrists, chest, and neck. They were not as bad as the sharp, swollen puncture marks, which were constantly itching and carved into her skin like knife wounds. The rash that erupted on the side of her neck and collarbone was the worst, yet Valerie was too afraid to ask for help.

Her heart pounding, she scratched a spot over the fabric just as Ethan leaned over and whispered in her ear, cracking his leather glove with the turn of his hand, "Please be courteous." His voice was warm and sweet, yet Valerie could not help seeing the constraint on his complexion.

The smell of pine and rotten fish filled her lungs when she slid her hand into his. The house was situated at the skirts of the open sea where boats frequently moored and the seamen roared unintelligible orders at their subordinates. Snow hid them from view, but Valerie could imagine their frostbitten faces, furrowed by the wash of sea salt and pale light, the staff unfurling weeds and fish net from the ships' sterns, wiping mist from their battered jackets and beads of sweat from their wool caps.

Lord and Lady Harker greeted them at the brightly colored, glass paned door with gracious smiles. Through the doorway, Valerie noticed the servants scurrying with trays in hand, and a string quartet and laughter spilled out of the drawing room and rang in her ears.

"Ah, Mr. Vertigo and Mrs. Vertigo, how wonderful to see you this evening! We are grateful for your presence," Cecilia Harker chirped with a shrill laugh that did not reach her eyes, pushing her tongue into the gap in her front teeth. Valerie returned the smile as the gentlemen huddled and exchanged nods in the corner. "How kind of you, Lady Harker. We're honored to be invited to your marvelous home."

As they silently walked through the long hall, Valerie silently studied her hostess. The dress was of indigo velvet brocade, the extravagant ruffled sleeves and boning on each seam gave Cecilia Harker a refined, tasteful look. Ribbon sashes and beadwork adorned its bodice, but it was the rhinestone brooch that really stood out against her jeweled chest. Her hair was softly pulled to the back of her head in a neat bun, dressed with feathers. She flipped open her large silk satin fan as she introduced Valerie to other guests. Gentlemen were sitting smoking at lounges at the far end of the room and the patch of smoke made it difficult to tell apart the faces.

"Ladies and gentlemen, may I have your attention? I would like to introduce a dear friend of mine, Lady Vertigo, who has graced us with her presence this evening. Mrs. Vertigo, please allow me to present to you the esteemed guests who have honored my home tonight. Lady Vertigo, these are my dear friends, Lady Catherine and Lady Amelia," Cecilia Harker said with a forced smile.

She placed a shaky smile on her lips and bobbed a curtsy before speaking. "Thank you, Mrs. Harker, for your warm welcome. I am most pleased to meet you," she turned to the ladies who looked up and down at her from their seats. An awareness of being scrutinized through smoke and whispered about dawned upon Valerie. A shiver ran through her spine as other guests left their seats and approached the table. Lady Amelia reminded her of a goat. Lady Catherine resembled a smallpox victim.

Cecilia Harker turned on her heels and gestured at a young man with a garish suit. "First, we have the dashing Lord Frederick, a renowned poet and a true connoisseur of the arts. I am most certain that his words can weave magic and transport you to distant lands."

Rose blotches appeared on Lord Frederick's cheeks, and he tried to look like he was fixing his cufflinks. He bowed slightly, opening his mouth to greet Valerie, but Mrs. Harker had already moved on to her next guest.

"Next, we have Lady Evelyn, a dear friend of mine, a woman of impeccable taste and a patroness of various charitable causes in our town and the surrounding area. Her passion for philanthropy knows no bounds."

Lady Evelyn smiled behind her fan which covered her mouth, so Valerie was not sure if what she saw was indeed a sincere one. She suspected she made careful notes of her appearance as the woman's eyes wandered over her. Her brows knitted together.

"Please allow me to introduce you to Sir Edward. One of the most distinguished scholars of our little town and a man of great intellect. We all consider ourselves lucky to have the opportunity to listen to his enlightening insights and knowledge."

A middle-aged man stepped forward with a smile, his grizzled hair shimmering under the refracted light from the crystals on the chandelier like iridescent feathers. Valerie gave a curt curtsy before turning to the last guest Mrs. Harker was pointing to.

"Lastly, we have Miss Karnstein. The renowned heiress of Karnstein estate and who graciously joined us a couple days ago due to the unfortunate snowfall. Nevertheless, we are ecstatic to find ourselves a friend in these marooned times."

Miss Karnstein idly extended her hand, and she shook it gently. "It is a pleasure to make your acquaintance," she said. Her labored breathing moved the tight, golden curls from her face. Despite her engaging smile, Valerie knew that she must have been sick, for her sallow complexion and dropped shoulders gave her a gaunt, skeletal look. Her maid probably tried her best to make her look presentable yet the dark shadows under her eyes gave her away. Her dark crimson bodice rose and fell in waves, accentuating her sickly pallor. Yet, there was a spark of energy in her eyes, a familiar understanding, like a welcome. There were no signs of flight in those eyes, bright and possessive, that Valerie felt like she had met the woman before. Something about her touch, the quality of her immense glance made Valerie shiver in equal dread and thrill. She was tall but not gaunt, it was almost comforting.

"Very pleased to meet you, Miss Karnstein," she murmured after a brief pause, and Mrs. Harker resumed her hostess duties. "If you would be so kind," she said, turning to her guests and slightly raising her voice, "could you escort Mrs. Vertigo to the dining room, Sir Frederick?"

"I am more than happy to oblige, madam," he bowed, and Valerie placed her hand on his elbow, shooting a furtive look at her husband, who was talking merrily with Sir Edward. Mrs. Harker carefully formed the pairs, mixing the couples to ensure a smooth discussion, and Valerie left the room with a knot in her stomach.

8

IT WAS NOT UNTIL Valerie slid into her cushioned seat that she realized how dilapidated and bare Vertigo Peaks was. Compared to the Harker manor-house, Vertigo Peaks looked like an abandoned, ancient-looking cottage. Everything was lit with a dim, intimate light. Even the gleam of the chandeliers was warmer, inviting. A glint of rings and lavish cutlery shifted with the embers of the fireplace. The long windows were draped in velvet curtains, a deep violet hue, the walls were adorned with hunting treasures and old family portraits, demonstrating the succession of family name clearly. Servants were rushing in and out of the room in silence, following a fixed path. A look of familiarity and habit had mellowed their faces and Valerie thought how natural it all seemed in this house, and noticed how labored and constrained her life looked in Vertigo Peaks. The musky smell of their rooms, the peeling wallpapers, the dust-covered furniture and the piles of old books and documents stacked in random corners with which her husband kept himself busy every waking moment. Vertigo Peaks was a dying man, carrying an irreparable loss on his hunched back whereas the Harker estate marked a great age, the corners of which rising steadily on the horizon, ready to put the hoary man to bed.

The knot in the pit of her stomach tightened. Between a sense of self-loss and unbelonging, she found herself wishing she was in a faraway place instead of sitting here and with these people, all laughing and jolly, their booming voices echoing in the long halls.

The dining room was buzzing with conversation. Ethan was at the far side of the table, next to Cecilia Harker, while other couples exchanged amusing remarks. Valerie, on the other hand, sat with her hands on her lap and kept her silence. She was not sure if he waited for her to start the conversation or if he was as embarrassed and uncomfortable as she was.

"So, Mrs. Vertigo," he began, after he served her soup with meticulous care and received no reply, "have you enjoyed your time in our town thus far?"

A guttural, sardonic laugh escaped her lips, but she managed to turn it into a polite smile before Lord Frederick took offense. "Indeed, Sir Frederick. I find it quite refreshing, even in this blustery and bleak weather." She stirred her soup, trying to keep her face expressionless.

"Surely, one cannot find much amidst the muddied paths and foul-smelling sea. The city, with its vibrant pulse and intellectual exchange, holds far more allure for a refined mind. Have you been to the city yet?" A flicker of passion passed his eyes. Valerie shook her head.

"I am afraid not. I must confess, although the city sounds delightful and charming, I am truly content here. I find the crowds and soirées to be somewhat exhausting. Don't you think a brisk walk under the open sky with only the howling wind for company is better? A solitary path, if taken with an open heart, can lead to the most exhilarating revelations, far grander than any drawing room soirée."

Sir Frederick choked into his napkin. He blinked; his composure completely lost. "A lady... walking, alone, in the wilderness? Mrs. Vertigo, that is simply not done! Think of the dangers—lurking ruffians, treacherous bogs, the utter lack of civilized conversation..."

He took a bite of his baked salmon and chewed it slowly, his brows knitted, his thin lips almost invisible. The mischievous glimmer disappeared from his eyes.

"My apologies... I did not mean to—" Valerie mumbled under her breath, trying to cover her mistake hastily, hoping he could not see the heat rising up her cheeks. But he was already distracted by Lady Catherine, who peered over his shoulder and gave her a glaring look. Poor, blundering Mrs. Vertigo. She could not even finish a conversation without embarrassing herself. She sniffed quietly, tears threatening to spill with a prickling sensation. She sat with her ears and neck burning, for the itch had returned, the swell of her neck, leaving a curdling sensation on her tongue.

Then, a soft voice, soft as falling snow, nothing more than a whisper, sliced through her brooding melancholy. "Mrs. Vertigo," it murmured, "I am very fond of walking myself. There's nothing more invigorating than a pleasant walk by a meadow, through the woods, on less trodden roads. That's such an admirable quality we women shall possess—venturing into the woods, into the night as we wish—despite the adversity and dire warnings of the opposite sex."

Valerie turned, surprised. Beside her sat Miss Mircalla Karnstein, extending her ungloved hand over the table to press hers. Her gaze still had that curious warmth, devoid of the disdain reserved for Valerie, and once again Valerie's head throbbed with the thought that she had met this woman before. The way her head swayed underneath the sparkling chandelier, her mouth formed a pleasant round shape, a blue vein bulged from her forehead alarmed her, prickling her skin. She moved restlessly in her seat, almost sighing under her cold touch. Perhaps it was her manner that intrigued her as for the first time that evening, the air around her felt lighter. Miss Karnstein's words, unlike the sharp barbs of animosity and gossip, had pierced through her sorrow, offering a glimpse of acceptance. This stranger saw not her isolation, but the embers of her spirit glowing beneath the ashes.

"Oh, please..." Valerie said, stumbling over her words, overwhelmed by her kindness. "You don't have to waste your pity on me, Miss Karnstein."

She sat up stiffly. A deep line creased Miss Karnstein's pallid forehead. She looked like a disturbed child, denied entry to a barred orchard, and Valerie was instantly filled with regret. Miss Karnstein uncurled her fingers from hers quietly. Valerie could see in the way she clutched her wine glass and moved it to her lips, the tightened shoulders, that she was hurt by her words. Yet, when she spoke, her voice did not bear a trace of harshness.

"My honesty has never been an act of charity, Lady Vertigo. It would grieve me the most if you believe so."

"Miss Karnstein—"

"Oh, but it's true," Miss Karnstein insisted, her gaze unwavering. "I admire you and rejoice in your quiet strength. You possess a resilience many of us could only dream of." She leaned forward. A fervent, milky look twisted her features while her anguish faded away with a movement of her hand. Did she know? Did she see her in the town, attacked and humiliated, shivering like a wet puppy? Valerie felt a blush rise to her cheeks, unbidden. No one had ever seen her that way, not through the layers of isolation and forced smiles.

The room remained oblivious to their conversation. The fire cracked while Mrs. Harker giggled with her guests, and her husband diligently cut his meat, nodding to whatever Mrs. Harker was saying. Just as Valerie opened her mouth to speak, one of the servants brought her dessert—a plum pudding. She was about to return Miss Karnstein's compliments when she caught sight of the servant. A young boy with a plain necktie, under which a dark stain had discolored its crisp whiteness. He cast an involuntary glance first. Then his eyes widened, and his hand flew to his throat in utter terror. Valerie was struck by a chilling sense of familiarity, dulled, yet still present, and the fragments of a dream—a nightmare, a haunting, a premonition—overtook her. She remembered the blood, the fall of snow, flakes gathering on his hair as he screamed. She gasped for breath as he stepped aside and moved the empty plates, noticing her surreptitious glance. Why did he hasten his steps, as if wanting to finish his job immediately so he could leave and talk to other servants about how the mistress of Vertigo Peaks had a hand in his suffering?

Valerie jumped to her feet. She had to stop him and talk to him. Maybe she could make him understand, persuade him or reason with him about what happened. But what happened? Her mind was a plane, bored with black holes, and she did not know what was real and what was a figment of her imagination. Maybe the boy stared because he recognized her from the town. She was Mrs. Vertigo, after all. It was not uncommon for people to look at her, or to follow her with hungry eyes whenever she stepped outside.

Now everyone was staring at her—including her husband—scowling and raising their brows, questioning—perhaps for the hundredth time—why an unremarkable character like her sat among them. Valerie felt lightheaded and rickety as the room spun and the walls moved.

"Mrs. Vertigo, are you alright?"

It was Miss Karnstein, half-turning in worry, but her voice sounded so distant, as though it was coming under the water. A spurt of bile filled her mouth. She moved away, not wanting to be touched, as Miss Karnstein's face crept closer.

"Lady Vertigo, you have been awfully quiet this evening. I hope I did not make the mistake of arranging a dinner party that would insult your merits."

Mrs. Harker was slurring her words, shrieking with utter haughtiness, her cheeks the same color as the port wine in front of her. She did not wait for Valerie to speak. "So, Mrs. Vertigo," she drawled, her voice laced with malice, "tell me once more, why you couldn't be bothered to follow a simple local ritual? You must have heard about the curse by now. Right, Mr. Vertigo?"

"My lady—"

Valerie sat down. She was still dizzy with her stomach lurching and blood pounding in her head. Why did not she leave her alone? Was it not enough that she was attacked and humiliated?

"Cecilia, dear, please—"

It was Mr. Harker, barely raising his voice, yet everybody heard him. He gently placed his fork to the side, the soft clink of metal echoing in the room, yet Mrs. Harker was unwilling to stop now that the dam of her mouth burst open, spilling all the venom she had carried long before Valerie arrived in this town.

"What your husband has not told you, madam," she said, stretching each syllable and her face a mask of repulsion, "is that if you do not produce an heir soon, your house will drag us into ruin. The curse will eat him alive first, then it will come for you. He started it all, and he must end it before it destroys us all."

"I don't understand," Valerie babbled. Everybody alluded to the curse, but she was yet to be illuminated about what it actually was.

She scoffed, jumping to her feet. Her chair fell with a thud. Others shifted uncomfortably in their seats but nobody dared to speak to her. Nobody moved. "I do not believe you do. I suppose you also don't know about Sir Ethan's dead sister, do you? Or the fact that people have been talking—they are telling me they saw the beast, that plague bearer, near your house. Our people are dying, hunted by a monster, because of your filthy family!" Her diamond earrings flounced as she spun to face Ethan. "You could not stand the silence in that house anymore, could you? Being alone, the guilt gnawing at your very being? Is that why you married her—to resurrect her image?"

He regarded her with an expressionless face, folding his arms. Yet there was a tinge of threat in his voice. "You overstep your bounds, Lady Harker. The particulars of my marriage are of no concern to you. My wife and I are very content."

"*Content*? A poor scullery maid at best, thrust into the lap of luxury, and expected to play the lady? I imagine contentment is rather a foreign concept to you. I bet you also entertain the idea that she is exceptionally *modest.*" Mrs. Harker made a sound between a snort and wheeze and pointed at Valerie. "She doesn't even know where to place her damned spoon and fork!"

"Cecilia, enough!" Mr. Harker banged his fist on the table.

Valerie looked down at the table. Miss Karnstein's spoon stood next to hers and her fork was on the opposite side. Likewise, Sir Frederick's knife faced hers. Valerie crumpled the tablecloth in her fist. She was seized with a sudden desire to jump on the table and dance, to cry, to laugh, and she became conscious of a stab of pain too, in the middle of her chest. She wished she was alone, away from this nonsense, not tormented by secrets and lies.

"You dare lecture me on manners?" Valerie hissed, her vision a blur. She rose again, threw her napkin to the surprise of Sir Frederick and Lady Catherine, who gave a small cry, and met Cecilia Harker's gaze with the tilt of her chin. "You, who has been spewing nastiness all evening, though I came to your house with an open hand? Your party might boast the finest china and crystal, but they wouldn't clean that tongue of yours. Will you lay your head tonight and congratulate your pathetic attempt to humiliate me in front of your dear friends? Will that clear your conscience?"

The last words spilled from her mouth with a quiver, and she stormed out in a huff. The last thing she saw was her husband's face, looking like a surprised owl. She swept past the guests, tears already rolling down her cheeks. She sought refuge in the moonlit garden, the crisp air biting at her tears and whipping at her skirts. If she weren't so sad, the landscape before her might have given her heart a relief. The snow, falling in thick flakes, painted the town in shades of gray, like thin sheets. Beyond the flickering lanterns and the billowing smoke, the jagged outlines of the peaks and the glimpses of the docks ribboned in front of her.

"Mrs. Vertigo!" a voice called then a cold hand touched her shoulder. She turned around, her eyes flashing, only to find Miss Karnstein gazing at her with utmost concern.

"Mrs. Vertigo," she whispered. "I was too stunned to speak. I am so sorry."

Valerie bit her lip, words catching in her throat, her itch burning even worse. "Please, just leave me alone."

"As you wish," Miss Karnstein replied, her voice low and firm, "but I want you to know that you did not deserve such harsh treatment. I was not familiar with Mrs. Harker's...Well...Let's say, questionable manners."

She took out a handkerchief, the initials of Miss Karnstein's name sewn in gold, and wiped from her cheek the tears. Valerie cried silently for a while; Miss Karnstein's palm pressed light against the small of her back. Her touch was just as cold as the wintry sky, sending a spark up through her spine. For a moment, she forgot she was standing outside the Harker estate. She forgot the drawn velvet curtains, the warmth of the fireplace, the gentle swing of the chandelier, the easy lilting quartet. There was only the soft brush of her thumb climbing up her waist, the steady beat of her heart beneath her palm, the familiar understanding in her eyes. Her cheeks were still ashen, not a touch of color flushing her skin, despite the brisk air. The snow had left soft peaks on her head, making her curls look like pastries.

"We better go back."

"Oh, I am sure they can manage without us."

"I cannot be quite so sure," Valerie replied, a hesitant smile tugging at her lips. "They might just fall apart from sheer boredom in the absence of their favorite subject. Their tongue might have grown brittle already."

Miss Karnstein chuckled, a sound so childlike and reverberating, her sharp teeth flashing in the moonlight. "I am afraid you might be right. Let's not keep them waiting, shall we? Imagine the disappointment if they discovered their evening's entertainment ran off to a moonlight rendezvous!"

She winked and Valerie could not help but laugh. And then she heard the sound of her husband calling her name.

"I guess this is my cue," Valerie said, unable to hide her disappointment. "Good night, Miss Karnstein."

Valerie thought Miss Karnstein seemed more effervescent and mischievous, not a trace of urgency in her voice, not gripped by a solemn farewell.

"Good night, Mrs. Vertigo."

9

WHEN VALERIE HEARD THE panting and sniffling down the dark hall, she was looking at the portrait of her husband's dead sister. The candlelight undulated, flickering precariously, and she was not so sure of what to make of last night when Ethan came into view. It was as if she aged overnight, seeing everything through a lens of unobscured hatred and pain. But on the other side, there was Miss Karnstein and their brief talk and the lines around her eyes when she laughed and the brush of her fingers on the small of her back. Valerie could not explain it. She found herself imagining the arc of Miss Karnstein's lips, dreaming about the way she comforted her, just standing there in the wind with her, listening and speaking with that soothing voice of hers, even as she called to her with sharp-edged teeth.

"I suppose I expected you to be here." Ethan said. Valerie shrugged her shoulders. Looking up at the portrait—lethargic, distant, beyond pain and fear—, she felt like fate played before her. The numbered days of her short life became more obvious, like a body of water one might pass through, bursting up like a spring.

It did not matter if she wanted to mend her relationship with the townspeople. It did not matter if she dragged herself up and down the peaks for forgiveness. It did not matter if her husband did not love her anymore.

"Do you remember the day when you proposed to me?" She asked. The calmness in her voice surprised even herself, entirely lulled by the unchanging absurdity of her situation. She had escaped the bear but fallen into the lion's den. Bloody, treacherous, complacent.

Ethan cleared his throat and Valerie could tell by his frown that she had reservations about talking about this particular topic. If hers was a path of guilt, biting at the core of her existence with a greater force she had never encountered before, then that would be her husband's path too. She was tired of bearing the burden thrown at her feet alone. If she was guilty, her husband was guilty too.

"I remember," she replied to the question herself, giving a sharp edge to her voice, playing with her ring. "You asked me if I could bear children. I said, 'Yes'. Then you asked me if I minded living far from home and I said, 'No'. I did not find it strange then. You only ask questions, digging the sole of your boot in the dirt, the white of your eyes obscured from view. It leaves me in shivers now. Were you frightened? You did not seem so. And perhaps that's the reason why I am thus broken. You chose me on purpose. The gullible, poor Valerie who always had an air of placid demeanor, who kept quiet when it mattered the most, who needed to get out of the falling apart cottage of her uncle, who would not dare refuse a sparkling stone on her finger and a high roof over her head. That's what you wanted all along: another portrait on your wall."

"Valerie—" he began, but his voice cut off in a piercing sound. He coughed into his fist, or so Valerie thought, but then he straightened up. Valerie noticed the pearl white handkerchief crumpled in his hand. She did not need to ask what the stain was. Blood trickled from the side of his mouth as he tried to wipe it again as best as he could, but there were already stains of dark crimson. Valerie stared at it, eyes widened, and he stared at her, his face sunken and blanched.

"What are you hiding from me? Why don't you tell me what happened to your sister? What is this curse everyone has been talking about?" she said, her voice a tremulous whisper.

"You don't know anything," he replied with a turn of his hand. He was bent over his stomach, groaning in pain, yet Valerie stood where she was, arms folded. "I can save us. I can save *you*. I can make it right this time. I didn't have a choice—I did what I had to do, even though he knew—why don't you just listen? If I lose this, her death will be for nothing. I'll lose everything." He threw his hands in exasperation.

"I've been listening to you ever since I set foot in this house! And all I've gotten in return, my dear, is riddles and abasement!"

"You don't know what it's like to spend your entire life trapped in this house! I have to live the rest of my days haunted by her, watch her as she turns blue. Over and over again, over and over... I never meant to do it... You have to believe me."

His gaze met hers, raw and desperate. A wild tangle of hair framed his contorted face, the guttering flames of his candles dancing on his figure. He raked his fingers through his hair, as if debating saying something else, yet thought better of it. He exhaled violently, a stricken sound, and a deep chill settled into Valerie's bones. What had he done?

"I don't want to be a part of this anymore," she said, bringing her hands to her chest, as if waiting for an attack. She did not know whether she was clinging to a shattered fragment of her marriage, or chased phantasms alongside her husband. Ethan's voice echoed through the hall, delirious as he slid down the wall, rocking back and forth, the back of his palms pressed against his eyes. Valerie did not hear the sobs at first, stunned by the nightmarish sight, yet they became louder and uncontrollable.

Suddenly he yelled from his corner like a caged animal, still deranged and convulsing with anguish. "No! You'll do as I say! I will not tolerate such insolence under my roof or so help me God, I'll send you back! Do you hear me?"

Valerie's stomach lurched. She did not want to look at him and see his eyes darting across her face, his scrawny neck slick with a halo of sweat.

"Till death do us part, husband." Valerie murmured with a bitter smile and stepped over him. And in the darkness, she made a vow: to confront the truth, whatever it may be, even if it meant staring into the abyss of Vertigo Peaks alone. The house quaked under her feet in response.

10

ETHAN HITCHED HIS SHOULDERS, the worn leather of his glove creaking in protest. Valerie saw his jaw clench and his lips twitch. He raised his hand to knock, but then hesitated. She could almost hear the gears in his mind turning—drawing a plan that would turn the tide and put him on the top again. It had been weeks since her husband's breakdown. It was the dead of winter, a perpetual sense of horror loomed in the air. It was almost January. The frost was thicker, the nights longer. It was not noon yet, but the sky was dark already, more snow looming on the horizon. Work was scarce, the growers were complaining about their winter crops, and all trade almost came to a halt like a frozen river. The doctor stopped by Vertigo Peaks every few days to report a case of plague or consulted with Ethan on how to proceed with the increasing number of deaths. It was possible to find a door marked with scarlet in every alley and a person wailing in front of it. With the hopes of mending what had happened in the Harker estate, Ethan had been working harder than ever before, visiting every destitute, spending hours and even days away from home.

The rasping coughs turned into a dry wheeze, and he rapped on the door. A moment passed then the door creaked open. A woman, her face etched with fatigue, stood before them. Valerie tightened her grip on Ethan's elbow. The doctor stepped forward, speaking in an unwavering voice.

"Good evening, Mrs. Harris."

She blinked slowly, as though she was trying to remember who they were, then a deep furrow appeared between her eyes. "Good evening," she replied tersely.

"May we come in?" The doctor raised his brows expectantly. The woman opened the door without a word, her lips pursed.

Valerie stepped inside, a wave of warmth washing over her, but it couldn't completely erase the chill that settled inside her bones. More disturbing than the cold, though, was the pungent, rancid smell that hung in the air. It reminded her of a butcher's shop, the kind that kept the rotting fat and offal and blood, leaving behind a sickly stench. It triggered a memory of damp linen and fevered brows, of nights spent fighting back nausea at her uncle's bedside.

She pressed on, following the woman down the narrow hall, the smell growing stronger with each step. It clung to the walls, seeped into the floorboards, a constant, unsettling reminder of what awaited them ahead. When they reached the room at the end, the source of the odor became clear. It swirled around a bed of straws like a cloud, emanating from the bowl of tissues discolored by pus. Ethan paused. Valerie shot a furtive glance at him, seeing his mustache bristle in the dim light of the room, then entered.

She could see the girl, propped up on pillows, her face ashen and eyes clamped shut. For a moment, Valerie thought she was dead. The arms were drawn up and crossed on her chest, which was devoid of any motion. Valerie's hand went up involuntarily and covered her mouth. The smell became almost too unbearable that she had to blink back her tears, her heart hammering against her chest.

They took another step, then another, until they stood beside the bed. This was not a face of the living; it was a face preparing to depart this hollow world. The veins on her fluttering eyelids were purple and blue, the corners of her mouth were curled as in a smile. Valerie had never seen a face so peaceful before. Without trouble or misery.

"How has she been doing, Mrs. Harris?" The doctor knelt beside the bed, reaching into his bag of bottles and bandages and other herbal treatments. Mrs. Harris sat on a chair at the foot of the bed, her fingers laced together on her lap and head hung low.

"Not getting any better."

The woman looked at them, eyes fixed on Ethan, burning with an anger that seemed to consume her from within. It was an anger born from helplessness, of watching her child wither away under the relentless grip of illness, an anger that found its way to her husband, for his muscles tensed beneath her gloved hands. She understood her rage, the likes of which had begun rooting in her body, the desperate need to find someone, anyone, to blame for the fast, agonizing decline of her daughter.

It was the plague. It was the beast. It had taken more lives ever since the townspeople confronted and accused them on that day. The doctor had informed them about the symptoms—fever, hysteria, loss of appetite and memory, lethargy, a strong dislike of light. The symptoms usually lasted for a fortnight before claiming the body. There was no cure or relief. The plague spread fast, by a bite the doctor believed, and the victim was not aware of the disease until it took them to bed. Already too late.

"It's not enough," Mrs. Harris said, her voice wavering at first. "These bottles, medications, balms of yours...They're just delaying the inevitable, aren't they?"

She grimaced at the bowl of bandages, a vein bulging on her forehead. The doctor lifted the thin sheet and placed the girl's hands on her side. If Valerie thought the smell was horrendous, the girl's wound was much worse. She followed the trail that climbed up the opening of the girl's dress. It was as if someone used her body as a canvas and splattered black ink all over her chest and chin. It was like looking at a leaf, the veins curling and uncurling on the skin. Two small drops of blood had dried around her neck. A muffled sound came from her throat, but nobody noticed.

The same puncture wounds, gaping and swollen, and the same rash. Though her rash had subsided quickly, the puncture marks were stubborn, and the itching had only gotten worse.

He sighed, his shoulders slumping lightly. His words hung in the air like a bad omen. "Mrs. Harris, I understand your frustration. We're doing everything we can, but this is a difficult case."

Mrs. Harris pointed a finger at her and Ethan, sounding unexpectedly rancorous, looking at their leather gloves, the thick shawls, and feathered hats. "It's difficult for us. Not for *you* now, eh?"

Later in the afternoon, after Valerie asked Ethel to fill up her basin and bring fresh towels then cleaned her wound alone, she sat in the parlor, cradling her teacup and taking a sip every now and then. A hush as thick as cobwebs had descended over Vertigo Peaks. The only light came from a log burning in the fireplace, casting long shadows that danced on the oak-paneled walls. The wind blew the snow and a distant smoke perched over the peaks.

She had been pondering if this was her end: miserable and excruciatingly gruesome. Who was she if not Mrs. Vertigo? What use would she have if she did not marry Ethan Vertigo? She was a nobody. Whether his ship hit the rocks or rang the sirens, she could not desert it. She was bound to remain in this town, at the skirts of Vertigo Peaks so long as she lived.

"The doctor wants to see you, madam."

Ethel was standing at the doorway, a troubled look on her face.

"Please let him in," she said. Her heart beat faster at the thought of him kneeling over patients, dead after dead, working his hands in a futile attempt. Even so, why did he want to see her? It had been weeks since he treated her wound from the attack. She had not asked for his services ever since. Valerie swallowed hard. Did he know about the puncture marks on her neck? Did she scratch it accidentally in front of him? No, it could not be. She was careful to cover the wound, not to touch it in front of people in an alarming way. She ran to the mirror to see if there was a stain, the slightest implication of blood, but the fabric was clean.

Ethel announced him as he took a few quick strides in her direction. He opened his mouth then closed it again, seeing Ethel waiting by the door for an order.

"You may leave Ethel." She turned to the doctor. His nervous hands held his chest tight, and a feverish look passed his eyes. His hair was tousled and if Valerie had not seen him a couple hours earlier, she would have thought he had been in some kind of a brawl. She gestured to one of the cushioned chairs and sat across from him, waiting for him to catch his breath.

The air, thick with the smell of snow and smoke, pressed against her, the silence broken only by the rhythmic rap of his boots against the wooden floor. "Are you going to tell me what happened, doctor?"

He tilted his face back, revealing his sweat-streaking and weary features, looking at her with a fearful eye. She was about to ring the bell and ask for help when he spoke, a raspy whisper. Valerie's head snapped up, her eyes darting across his face like a startled animal's.

"She's dead, Mrs. Vertigo. I-I could not save her. She died screaming," he said, looking at his hands. "Her heart stopped beating beneath my palms. I did not know what to do. I could only watch as she went stiff."

The girl was dead. All the color drained from his face. He burst out crying, his head in his hands, his shoulders shaking violently. His composure crumbled before her eyes; the man she had known to be serene by nature had vanished. Finally, he stopped sobbing and lifted his head slowly, his eyes red-rimmed and haunted. The tears were replaced by a dark, indecipherable pain.

"Forgive me, madam—" He stuttered. "I did not mean to trouble you with my duties, or rather, my failures. It is not the reason why I am here," he said, pulling out a small piece of paper from his waistcoat and examining it. He looked at the paper for a moment, then his features hardened, a steely glint in his eyes. Valerie's heart lurched. She held her breath, her blood heavy like lead in her veins. As he unfolded it, his face leeched even further, as though the paper was sucking the lifeblood out of him.

He whirled towards her, his eyes wide with fury she had never witnessed before. He held her gaze as an object of scorn, but before she could ask him what the note said, a thunderous banging from the front door erupted the silence. The snow outside had seemed to recoil, then resumed its assault with a renewed force. Valerie jumped in her seat and the doctor shot her a panicked glance. A minute later, Ethel appeared in the doorway again, out of breath.

"A lady wants to see you, madam," she said. "I told her that you are busy at the moment, but she insisted on talking to you."

"Well, go on then. Call for the lady," Valerie said, raising a brow. Ethel was still lingering in the doorway. Her face reddened; she hid her hands under her apron then adjusted her cap. "Who is she, Ethel?"

"Erm...The lady...Madam..." Valerie noticed her surreptitious glance down the long hall, as though she wished the lady to appear behind her so she would not have to embarrass herself for uttering the words. When nobody came for her rescue, she shrugged her shoulders. After clearing her throat, she said, "The lady refuses to come inside the house or give her name unless you talk to her first."

Then, suddenly, she added these words: "The lady looked incredibly morbid and hysterical, madam, much too sick I think." Valerie pursed her lips but tried to keep a posture of repose in front of the doctor who was now watching her with a mixture of anxiety and weariness.

"What do you think, doctor? Ethel says the lady looks sick. Is the plague...the disease contagious? Should I let her in?" Her words trailed off in a whisper. The doctor stood up, his face still austere, yet gave her a sympathetic smile and walked to the door with her.

"The disease seems to only affect the bitten person, madam. I have not yet come across any evidence that it is contagious."

Because patients don't live that long, Valerie thought with a shudder.

Ethel led the way in silence. Valerie staggered to the door, the doctor's strained breath on her back, only to find a whimpering woman, cloaked in burgundy. The flurry of snow blurred the tall figure. Valerie put her arms around herself and retreated a few steps back. The road to the town was hidden from view and the wind was beating against the stone walls of Vertigo Peaks. An impassable wasteland, yet someone dared to brave it. All she saw was the fluttering cape like a rose bloomed too soon. First, the gleam in the woman's eyes shot forward, then emerged her stricken face.

"Mrs. Vertigo," she stammered. "Please, help me."

For a moment, a jolt of recognition and excitement coursed through her veins. Valerie would recognize the voice even if she were half the world away, its cadence engraved in her mind without a reason or deliberation. She did not understand how it happened or why, but when she called her name, a familiar, sweet ache already claimed a place in her heart.

"Miss Karnstein," she gasped.

II

"GOOD HEAVENS! WHAT ARE you doing out in this weather?" Valerie mumbled, then quickly added, "Please come in." The heavy oak door creaked open, and Miss Karnstein entered, hair wild, eyes full of tears, snowflakes at the tip of her lashes. "My carriage broke down and I haven't heard from the coachman ever since. I—" She drew in a shaky breath and Valerie suspected she was about to burst into tears, but she composed herself. A wistful expression flickered across her face, one mingled with apprehension. The faint pallor of her cheeks twisted Valerie's stomach as she said, "I cannot go home. All the roads are blocked. I really have no place to go."

Seeing Valerie and Ethel completely still, the doctor stepped forward and offered his hand to Miss Karnstein and rammed the door shut. "Come in, miss. You'll freeze out here. Ethel, bring something warm to drink."

Ethel raised both her eyebrows to her hairline, her eyes darting from the doctor to Valerie, as he ushered them to the drawing room. Valerie was truly dumbfounded, continuing to stare at this unexpected guest as her skirts swept the hall and the glow of candles flickered on her face. The doctor led her towards the fire, yet she did not seem to shiver. Valerie could see the purple hue on her nails, her chapped lips, but her chest rose and fell in regular intervals. "Just caught the tail end of that blizzard, let's hope," the doctor said, his voice a welcome intrusion to the crackling fire and swirling snow.

Ethel returned, bearing warm towels and a steaming mug of spiced tea. Miss Karnstein accepted it with a grateful smile. As she sipped, Valerie watched her, taking in the details: the way her eyes narrowed when she raised the cup to her lips, the sparks that danced in her gaze, the familiar astonishment. She realized Miss Karnstein did not want to be here. It was the same grievous expression Valerie wore ever since her wedding night, the same stiffness betraying the calm air that hung around her. Something in her stomach clenched.

If there was one thing she had learned from her uncle's wrath, it was survival. It did not take long for her as a child to learn that she had to mix herself in the patterns of her uncle who took away her supper because she failed to complete her chores, made her spend hours outside until the sun went down because she did not wake up before dawn. Want to deserve a hot bowl of soup? Do whatever the uncle says. Is it better to try to warm your fingers under the cold blanket instead of spending the night in the barn? Then don't go against his word. Therefore, she quickly made a habit of staying out of her husband's business and did what she was told when she got married.

Similarly, it did not take long to realize that this would not save her from animosity or violence. She had to adapt, morph herself once more, in order to survive. She cut out some of the parts that made people frown, bit the tip of her tongue that made her husband rasp. Granted, she did not do a great job, but Ethan was not a man of many desires. He burned with a single desire: to keep this barren town in line. In these trying times, having Miss Karnstein on his side would greatly benefit him. And her. Especially after the dinner party fiasco.

"Let me have a look, miss," the doctor said. Miss Karnstein allowed him to take her pulse, check her temperature. Valerie's fingers tightened around her ring. The doctor stepped back. "No fever, madam," he finally said with cloudy eyes, his forehead creased in thought, pointing at Miss Karnstein. "Pulse is abnormally irregular. Just the shock, I suspect. A warm fire, a good night's sleep, and Ethel's chick soup tomorrow should suffice. You'll be right as rain."

"You are most welcome to stay," Valerie said. She sounded like it was hard to find the right words. "This weather is not fit for travel."

Miss Karnstein hesitated, and a nervousness washed over her face. "I wouldn't want to impose, Mrs. Vertigo," she replied, raising the cup to her lips again.

Valerie smiled. A thrill rushed through her body. She did not know the loneliness in her was thus enormous, rendering her this vulnerable and eager. "Nonsense. Think of it as reprieve from the snow, a chance to rest and gather your bearings. We have plenty of room in Vertigo Peaks."

The truth was, Valerie craved her company. Not just for the entertainment of a new face, but for the glimpse Miss Karnstein offered into what Valerie thought long dead within her.

"Besides," she added, her voice tinged with mischief and laughter, "who knows when the roads will be passable again? You are stuck here, at my mercy, as it were."

Miss Karnstein's lips curled into a beaming smile and Valerie saw there was a hint of amusement, perhaps even affection, written on her face. "Then I guess I have no choice but to accept your offer, my lady," she replied.

In the most unexpected way, she was glad to admit that it was relief melting her fears, hearing Miss Karnstein's warm voice. For the first time in months, she felt alive, not just with, but with the promise of something new. As Valerie led her upstairs, her hand brushing hers on the banister, a strange sense of calm settled within her. Miss Karnstein's name hung between her lips, unspoken yet sweet, stirring something dormant within her.

12

MISS KARNSTEIN'S CHAMBER WAS a cozy one, located in the same wing as her own. She had chosen this room because it was relatively fair and decent compared to the ones on the other wing; its windows overlooked the edge of the forest, and Miss Karnstein could easily send word if anything was disagreeable or troublesome. Yet, here, in this secluded part of the manor-house, even the air reeked of forgotten things—a blend of dust, damp parchments, and a faint undercurrent of something oily that clung the back of Valerie's throat like cobwebs.

Linen sheets, once pristine and starched, now coiled in a tangled heap atop a cot. The candlelight, if it could be called such, dared not venture far past the threshold, which left them in the dark for several minutes before Ethel aired the room and placed new candles in an iron candelabrum, casting long shadows across the scene. Each flicker danced across the grimy walls, conjuring monstrous shapes from the damp and peeling wallpaper. There was a chilly, musty smell when they entered. The cramped bookshelves were full of old books, their warped spines and leather bindings bulging with arcane symbols that Valerie had never seen before.

She was filled with sudden dread and shame, for this was not a room fit for a guest, yet Valerie was not sure whether other rooms would be in better condition. She turned and hid the blush on her cheeks in the candlelight, speaking in a flat tone.

"My apologies for the state of the room. We were not really expecting a guest."

"Nonsense. It's much better than spending the night in the snow and risking freezing to death."

Valerie watched her guest with keen eyes. The initial stiffness gone, Miss Karnstein resembled when she met her at the dinner party. Valerie could see her clearly now. She moved with the trained elasticity of a young woman; the softness in her voice and the lightness of her step strangely reminded Valerie of herself. Nevertheless, in some moments—the nature of which was always fleeting and elusive—Valerie thought she held herself back. Her eyes remained guarded, her words constrained, and Valerie found herself wanting to probe the reaches of her mind, lay it bare and strip its secretive nature for reflection.

"Tell me, Miss Karnstein, how did you manage to escape the blizzard unscathed? Not many souls brave the storm on foot."

Miss Karnstein did not look away, but the ghost of a smile played at her lips. "I did not have to walk very far, Mrs. Vertigo. I don't think I would have made it to your house if that was the case. A bit of wilderness wisdom sufficed."

"Ah, I see. Tell me where does your family hail from? I'm afraid we skipped a formal introduction because of my..." Valerie's voice trailed off.

Miss Karnstein sat on her bed, lazily playing with the sheets, her gaze intent on Valerie. "Up from the North. A rather remote, uninteresting village, I think." She then raised a brow, chuckling. Valerie could not help but picture her with a glass of wine in her hand, relaying the journey of her life to her awed audience. "Perhaps I'm simply too adept in blending in, so people either take my presence for granted or do not acknowledge it at all."

The answer, while polite, was evasive. Still, Valerie flushed a bit at her nonchalant remark, embarrassed once more. She decided to change the subject. "And your carriage," she asked, "Did you find help, or..."

"Sadly, beyond repair," Miss Karnstein interrupted, a touch of wistfulness in her voice. "But thankfully, your hospitality renders that loss a mere inconvenience."

Valerie lingered by the bed, her heart pounding in her throat, and smoothed the creases on her skirt because she did not know what to do with her hands. "I must confess, your companionship was the only thing I was aware of that night, the pure bliss I now have the chance of reminiscing about."

Miss Karnstein turned, and their eyes met and something inside her ribs stirred. "I must confess, our conversation was the only thing worth staying for."

Ethel burst into the room with a clean set of sheets and a nightgown in her hands, and when she saw them, she muttered an apology. Valerie stepped back, her face burning, as if she had just admitted a crime. She had lost track of time. Darkness had swallowed the room whole and only a candle stood alight. It was so much colder than it had been in the evening.

"Please light the fire and use oak. It burns the longest, so it will keep our guest warm for the night. Prepare the chicken soup as well."

She left the room without another word, wringing her hands, and her heart was beating like it might rip her chest apart.

In the night, the woman came back crawling. Her hands slipped under the quilt, a trail of blood following her, and she bore a touch that was familiar yet cold, creeping up her legs. Valerie was seized by a heavy and cloying sense of agony when the woman pulled up her skirts, climbing up her thighs. She lay pinned on the sheets drenched in her sweat, and her moan echoed in the vast emptiness of her room.

She shuddered, not from fear, but from a nameless yearning that clawed at her stomach. She saw, or fancied seeing, a blank, featureless face like a clean slate, except that the features quickly arranged themselves into Mircalla Karnstein's pallid countenance as Valerie had seen her last. Her loose curls brushed Valerie's cheeks as she climbed on her, her gaze sharp as a blade, and a pair of scarlet eyes narrowed on her, a bottomless hunger reflecting the moon. She wanted to say her name but her mouth was tightly closed as if sewn shut.

Miss Karnstein traced the quickened pulse at her throat, then she leaned in, and Valerie felt a sudden twinge on her breast, followed by a sense of strangulation. Valerie's whole body went numb, sending a searing fire through her veins, arching into Miss Karnstein's demanding touch.

And then, as swiftly as it began, it was over. The night stretched before her without limits, Valerie in the center of it. Mircalla Karnstein pulled away, leaving behind another set of puncture wounds on her skin. A moan, half-sob, half-shiver escaped Valerie's parched lips. She was agony, she was sweet ecstasy, she was the spark of defiance, akin to a forbidden desire, Valerie had been craving.

Valerie awoke to the sound of her screaming. The candle was guttering out. She stirred the embers in the hearth, watching the sparks dance. Beneath her nightgown, her fingers reached for her neck first, running a finger over the scab on her neck. She then moved a little lower, feeling her heartbeat under her palm. Black spots flooded her periphery when she touched the fresh puncture marks, still bleeding, hot and throbbing. The mark of a beast. She was afraid of closing her eyes and picturing that blank face that nefariously took the shape of Miss Karnstein.

13

THE SCENE OF PAIN was still there, at the crack of dawn, when Valerie began to rouse, shivering; the searing kiss piercing her breast, the blood-soaked hands wandering up her thighs, the loose curls caressing her cheeks, and Miss Karnstein swelled from it. She was perplexed by it all as she pressed cotton pads to her wound. It was a ghastly side, she thought, worse than she'd imagine. A part of her flesh was pulled away and feeling queasy, she could not examine it further. She grunted as she rose and lit a new candle, walking down the dark hall with a new resolution.

She wanted to look at Miss Karnstein, study her face for signs of disturbance and grotesque attitudes. It was just an easy way to put her nightmare-ridden mind at ease without causing any embarrassment. Her husband would laugh at her story but what scared her was the doctor. It was possible that he would treat it as a fanciful notion, a disquieting effect, yet a part of her knew that he would be alarmed, for the wounds could be taken as the sign of the plague that ravaged their town. She was not in excruciating pain, so it seemed pointless to alarm him.

Valerie knocked on Miss Karnstein's door softly, afraid of waking her up, yet still too conscious of decorum for some weird reason, then twisted the knob. The door creaked but did not open. "It's most strange," Valerie whispered to herself and tried again, this time pushing it harder in vain. It was locked. She put her ear to the door and listened for any sound that Miss Karnstein might have roused, stirring up in her bed. Nothing but a dead silence upon the air.

Miss Karnstein did not come down for breakfast. Valerie wiped a rolling bead of sweat off her brow before she reached for the butter. Ethan did not seem to notice the absence of his guest nor was he paying particular attention to the presence of it. With a sigh, she turned to her husband who was scribbling furiously on a yellow sheet of paper, his head bowed.

"The state of the weather is absolutely awful," she began with a shaky voice. Accepting a stranger into the house seemed less sensible now. "I wonder how long it'll stay like this."

Ethan nodded without looking up, puffing away at his cigar. Valerie fidgeted in her seat.

"Are winters always this harsh here? Nothing but snow for months on end? I am asking because..." She trailed off, a lump forming in her throat as Ethan looked up, his pen in the air.

"Yes?" he said, sounding like he was very bored. Valerie spread another thick layer of butter on her bread. Her fingers were all sticky.

"Well...Do you remember Miss Karnstein? From Mrs. Harker's dinner party?"

He put down his pen, wiping the ink off with a crisp white handkerchief. He wrinkled his nose, as if the room were thick with stink. "I'm afraid not," he said at last.

"Lady Karnstein kindly requested our help as her carriage unfortunately broke down in the middle of the storm yesterday. She arrived here on foot, poor thing, rattled and freezing. The doctor advised a good night's rest, so I insisted she spend the night here."

"And?" His brows arched to the hairline, puffing on his cigar slowly.

"I just-I just thought maybe her presence can be of assistance to our... *situation*. It doesn't look like the weather will begin to turn anytime soon."

He tilted his head on one side to study her, eyes narrowed behind a smoky film. "You need not concern yourself with the matter. If you're longing for a close confidante to liven up the wintry days, just say so. I am not fond of word games."

"Yes, dear," Valerie replied. She had lost her appetite. She was startled when he spoke again. He was not looking at her, buried in his work again, yet his voice floated in the air, seeping through her body like spilled ink.

"I am aware that I did not do a proper job of fulfilling my duties as a husband. My expectations might have exceeded your..." He paused for a better word then puffed another cloud, "knowledge. Let us be tolerable, shall we?"

"Of course," she said, almost choking on her tea. She was already used to her husband's formal speeches and indifferent words of reproach, but this was the first time he was expressing a sense of regret and guilt to her. She remembered their conversation in front of his sister's portrait, the way he shrank into himself like a sick, old man. That was the first time she had the courage to speak what she had been thinking. Perhaps this helped Ethan look at things objectively.

"Miss Karnstein may stay as long as she wants," he added. Only did he glanced at her after folding the paper, eyes shining with what she could have sworn was wickedness before he smiled at her.

The clock had just struck two in the afternoon when Miss Karnstein joined her in the parlor.

"Miss Karnstein!" Valerie sat up, leaping on the sofa in shock. "I came to your room to wake you up, but the door was locked. I was beginning to worry that you had left the house. Why don't you sit down and enjoy a good meal?"

She was about to ring her bell when Miss Karnstein raised her hand in opposition. She tried to smile, but the effort contorted her expression into a slight pout. Her eyelids fluttered, a grimace escaping her mouth, and Valerie noticed her languid mood. There was no trace of her lively countenance, all Valerie saw was an impression of a shadow walking towards her. Her hair was tousled, hanging loosely around her waist with copper streaks at its tips, like she had strayed into the deep woods at night. Her nightgown in disarray, Miss Karnstein trudged over to the closest chair and let out a deep sigh.

If Valerie was anxious before, it was nothing to what she felt right now. "Miss Karnstein," she cried, springing up and rushing to her side. The effort exhausted her, she pressed her hand over her eyes and did not speak. Her lips were almost invisible, a violet thin line like an incision. Her nails, Valerie noticed, were filled with dirt.

She swallowed and said, "I'll send someone to call for the doctor." She pressed a hand on her feverish cheek, coated with cold sweat. "You're burning."

Miss Karnstein tightly clutched at her wrist with a shriek of terror. Her face underwent a change, losing her original lapping sweetness, that struck Valerie with horror for a moment. The pressure of her fingers turned Valerie's wrist white as milk. She was not the weakling she was a moment ago. Her thin face was overclouded, livid with a force that Valerie did not recognize, staring at her and baring her sharp teeth, a spirited likeness to a trapped animal.

"No," she cried again. "I shall not let this doctor of yours examine me again." She added hastily, "It would be considered improper. It must be the cold, Mrs. Vertigo. A longer rest should do me good."

Valerie could not understand why she was so vehemently opposed to seeing the doctor, especially after she let her take her pulse yesterday. She did not say anything so as not to offend her guest but it was all strange, almost comical, and Valerie returned to her seat in thought. Miss Karnstein had the same languor of the infected townspeople, and although Valerie did not see any scars, she began to think that Miss Karnstein had contracted the disease as well.

Betraying her hospitality, she entreated her guest to be examined again, yet did not receive a response. "Would you like to return to your bed?" Valerie at last asked, numb with the tedium of the moment. Miss Karnstein looked up, the circles under her eyes strikingly dark, and nodded. Valerie helped her get up, throwing her arm over her shoulder, and carried her upstairs.

The candles were still burning at her bedside and the bed itself was untouched. Miss Karnstein's chest was heaving and Valerie tossed the quilts aside to control the fever. She soaked a towel in the basin and wiped away the trickling sweat. A few stray curls stuck to her forehead, damp and slick, so Valerie moved the wet towel over them. The flickering eyelids opened, translucent and blue, and her lips softened.

"You scared me so much, Miss Karnstein! Drink this." Valerie held the base of the glass to help and she took two quick sips. "Are you feeling better?"

"It's passing now," she closed her eyes and murmured, more to herself than Valerie, as her head fell onto the pillow. She noticed Miss Karnstein's hand reaching for her over the sheet. Her heart racing, she held her fingers in hers. There was a melancholy on her face that softened her features and Valerie realized how beautiful and winning she was. It was not just the golden curls or the bow of her lips. Something lingered beneath that surface, attractive and almost alarming.

"Are you with me, Mrs. Vertigo?"

"Yes, Miss Karnstein, I am."

Valerie did not know why tears pricked her eyes or why a flood of relief washed over her whenever Miss Karnstein's chest rose and fell, but the thought of losing this woman she had yet to know dearly tormented her. She wanted to talk to her just as they did at the dinner party, to get lost under the spell of her soothing words. How could she ever describe this tantalizing, fearless hope of knowing someone for the first time and falling in love with them? For this was love, surely, not in the shape of a lover, but shooting forth unexpectedly like grass among the cracked stones. It was a healing balm that Valerie needed all these months, passing in a blur of hurt. It was a beloved soul who sought her because she knew she was made alike with the desperate desire to belong. To somewhere, to someone.

"I saw you in a dream last night," Valerie said in a hoarse whisper. "You came to me and I awoke in my bed. I watched you in horror as you climbed on my bed. It was the most strange occurrence because then, I dreamt not. It was cold. You were with me when the deepest agony pierced through me."

"I saw you in my dream too." She sat up, blinking slowly. "You were looking at me and I held you as you cried."

"How wonderful and strange! The face was a blank slate at first, then I made out the hazy outline of your face like fragments falling into place. I wanted to call out your name, ask why you visited me but I could not speak. I am most certain you sank your teeth into my flesh. Then I was bound with a woe so unfathomable that I forgot where I was. If it did not hurt me so much, I would have found it very amusing!"

"What did you do then?" Miss Karnstein asked, a flash of fire in her eyes. She gave her hand a tight squeeze.

"I came to myself in complete darkness, I think." Valerie did not want to admit she was looking at her wound in the mirror. There was no use further troubling the sick woman. She scratched the spot where the cotton pad was. A hint of a smile tugged at Miss Karnstein's lips. Valerie could see her teeth flare through the opening of her mouth.

She then replied, "Were you afraid? I shall be miserable if you had felt so." Valerie believed that the memory pained her, and also there was something of a bursting candor that enthralled her. Her eyes did not stray from her face as she shook her head. "I was not afraid. I was glad, for I believed I found a friend."

Miss Karnstein's eyes welled with tears. Valerie wiped them away with the towel in her hand.

For someone like her who grew up in the shades of loneliness, this confidence, this fondness was almost suffocating. She thought she could do nothing but accept and grow this affection within her, and though unexpected, carry it with grace. Miss Karnstein sank into her pillow with a sigh, still holding her hand.

14

THE NEXT FEW DAYS were spent with Ethel bringing in fresh linen, steaming soup, and buckets of water, and Valerie sitting at the end of the bed, chatting with Miss Karnstein. December was in full swing. It was an unending period of frosted panes, reddened cheeks, eyes swollen by sleep, and an absolute quietude. She wanted forgiveness, an idyllic existence; she wanted the crunch of her footsteps on the frozen ground, vapor curling around her mouth, security. The blizzard had gotten worse and the snow still fell, severing their connection with the town entirely.

One of those days when it was impossible to realize the passage of time and the mind was untroubled by the prospect of adventure, Valerie found Ethel helping Miss Karnstein change into a new nightgown. Ovals of sweat had left a blot on the back of the dress, shaped like a shallow lake, but the gray, deathly pallor had disappeared from her face. She was standing on her own, leaning on her bedpost, and staring out at the thick clouds of the wintry air with a serene look on her face.

Valerie stepped in. "I'll take it from here."

Ethel turned to her with an unfocused expression and disappeared in the hall with a quick bow of her head. The room, affected by the encrusted, moldy wallpapers and moth-eaten books, was already sultry and almost oppressive, and smelled like something had died or decayed. The air lay completely putrid, so Valerie cracked a window open to let the crisp air in.

"You must be feeling much better," said Valerie in a low voice, "I'm glad to see you up."

Miss Karnstein lifted her gaze to look at her, two smoky specks dimmed by sickness, and Valerie could see her smile, careless, clairvoyant, and light, bringing a spot of rose on her lips. It was so easy to picture her as happy, for her temperament was naturally sanguine and independent, and if not for her sickness, Valerie could easily attest to her charm. Yet, seeing her all dull and bruised, she shifted uneasily before her, struggling to carry on with the conversation.

"I'm sure you will be rid of this cold in no time," she murmured. "Your family must be distressed by your absence and I am a terrible host for not having noticed it. But you can send them a short note, weather permitting. I'll see to it."

Miss Karnstein's face tightened, her head low, the mouth compressed. "Please do not trouble yourselves in this harsh weather. I'm sure they know by now that I won't be coming home soon and that communication would be impossible."

"But you must let them know you're safe and well! I cannot accept leaving your family with such terrible uncertainty!" Valerie pulled a yellowed piece of paper amongst the old books. "I will personally help you write the note, I do not want you to exhaust yourself. What is your address? There will be a stagecoach leaving tomorrow, I think. We can absolutely make it by then."

Suddenly, Miss Karnstein screamed a loud, shrill cry, then she gasped, again and again. Her voice was too strange, too deep. "I do not want to write a note to my family," she said, almost hissing, then she wept with hysteria. "They must not know I'm here. If they find out I'm taking this journey on my own..."

She closed the distance between them and threw herself into Valerie's arms. "Please promise me you won't contact my family and put me in great danger. If not..." She pulled herself away from Valerie's embrace, her cheeks glistening with tears. "I will leave your house at this very moment and never get in your way again."

Valerie reeled back, her heart leaping up in her throat. "But Miss Karnstein..." She cut her off.

"I know that I have not given you the answers you deserve, that I keep you in the dark and want you to trust me regardless. You and your husband welcomed me to this wondrous place very kindly and handled my illness skillfully, despite my rejections for examination, but it would devastate me if I made you carry my burden."

"Please, Miss Karnstein. I'd hate to see you in anguish. I absolutely have no interest in judging or exacerbating your situation. I was just trying to help, and if my silence is the only instrument that will keep you safe here in this bitter winter, I'll gladly do so. I am sorry."

"Ah, Mrs. Vertigo. I'm forever indebted to you. Thank you."

Miss Karnstein wrapped her hands around Valerie again, pressing her chin into the crook of her neck. Valerie stared, breathless, at the top of her head. For a moment, she wished she could bury her nose in Miss Karnstein's hair, disguise herself beneath the sheen of her loose curls, now clean from those coppery streaks and soft like velvet, with no hurry, no bounds. She felt expansive and inclined to talk. Now words were washing over her, words that she did not think she had known, perched at the roof of her mouth with delight and pride. She did not want to lose this newfound friendship. It was as if what was missing came back to her, bolder and better, and she had ignored the gnawing sense of danger in the back of her mind, telling her that Miss Karnstein was sick with plague.

Miss Karnstein gestured at the new nightgown. Valerie remembered why she had come into the room and blushed, taking the dress from her hands.

"So you liked Vertigo Peaks?" Valerie asked as she pulled the nightgown over her head and fastened the buttons. The dress was nothing elegant, high-collared with ruffles at the cuffs, yet only "beautiful" came to Valerie's mind to describe her guest in it. She paused when she reached her waist. She felt her neck redden with a familiar prickling sensation and stepped back, letting her guest handle the rest of the buttons.

There was a momentary tremor in Miss Karnstein's voice. "Certainly. I was in a very dark place before, like I was at the bottom of a well. Damp and cold. This place reminds me that I can heal."

"Of course!" She looked at her guest, incredulous. "I shall ban you from speaking such hopeless words."

The sound of her laughter echoed in the room. Then there was more laughter, Valerie herself laughing too. She loved the clatter they made. She was coming to recognize it as something rare and unwonted which filled her heart with warmth, as though she were a seedling waiting for spring.

"Thank you again, Mrs. Vertigo," Miss Karnstein said, climbing on her bed and covering her trembling legs with the quilts. "I am only grateful for your generosity, for taking care of me even though I am but a stranger to you."

"We'll have plenty of time to remedy that foreignness. You and I will see each other quite often, Miss Karnstein and I'm afraid I'll take the risk of making you sick of me since you are stuck with me for a while after all."

A faint smile lingered and bared her sharp teeth again. "Please call me Mircalla," she said, or rather demanded. "I'm quite content with keeping your company." Although a thick frown pressed around her brows and a shadow crossed her face every now and then, those did not stay long as they melted into a welcoming smile whenever Valerie spoke.

But the nights were drawing in fast, and the promise of a friend became too much to bear at once. The house groaned. She stood in the threshold, instructing her guest to rest well then closed the door.

15

"There's a note for you madam." Ethel approached Valerie, the grating click of her heels giving her a headache. She tore the envelope open and moved closer to the fireplace. A dark noon lay outside, with a heavy snow, raining soot and grime, but it looked more like a gray dusk settling on the peaks.

Valerie read the note then read it again. The handwriting, which was penned in cursive, was hasty and smudged, almost illegible, yet there was no doubt that it was her husband's writing. She sat up in her seat, scratching her cheek uncomfortably, as if humiliated by the letters. "My husband says he is snowed in and all the roads to the town are blocked. He does not know when they will clear the road."

"Yes, madam. We did not get fresh milk delivery today. It's like the crack of doom outside."

Valerie gave her an anxious look. Ethel waved her hands, which she had hid under her apron, as if to soothe her. "Do not vex yourself, my lady. We have enough food and coal for weeks, thankfully."

"Good afternoon, my lady."

Valerie's eyes widened when she saw Miss Karnstein approaching. The waxy and sallow hue on her face had disappeared from her face and the sparks in her eyes made her look even more youthful. Her cheeks were still pale, yet she looked healthy in her green dress. The symmetry of her face was intimidating at first glance, but when she passed her seat Valerie recognized a waft of her civet perfume and smiled. Her hair did not hang about her in loose curls as before; instead, it was pinned up in a wide bun on top of her head.

"It's actually twelve o'clock," Valerie said in exasperation and turned to her guest. "What a dreadful scene! My husband informs us that he's snowed in and the roads are blocked. He also says he'll send the doctor to gather a couple belongings as soon as the weather permits. One would expect the business endeavors to slow down in this season, yet he seems determined to work."

"Indeed," her guest replied, nodding absentmindedly. "This doctor of yours..." Miss Karnstein began after a brief pause, a most peculiar and questioning lilt in her voice, "He seems to help him a great deal. Is he one of your servants as well?"

Valerie did not know what to say. She turned her attention to her cross-stitch. For some reason, talking about the doctor made a twinge of unease pass through her. He had a furious look about him when they last met and Valerie did not get another chance to talk about that piece of paper after the sad demise of one of his patients. What was in it that should concern her?

"I apologize if I overstepped my bounds," Miss Karnstein said.

"No, it's alright. He's one of my husband's best friends and a very adept doctor, that's all."

"I see. I haven't had the opportunity to chat with Sir Ethan yet, but it's clear that he is dedicated to this town. You must be proud of him, Mrs. Vertigo."

"Miss Karnstein, I'd rather talk about something else if you'd be so kind."

Valerie fidgeted in her seat, the glint of her wedding ring blinding her for a moment. That was pitiful. Her guest did not have a clue about the turmoil shaking the town. She did not know her humiliation or her husband's obsession for absolute power. She did not know Vertigo Peaks was crumbling around them. Why did she feel compelled to hide everything? Wasn't this the same secrecy that condemned her to isolation? Had it not made the townspeople hostile to her when all she wanted was a happy marriage? If, she thought, a loveless face was all she could see, was it not her right to look away?

She gripped her hand to steady a tremor and tried to find her calm voice. "I don't know what I'm doing wrong but our marriage is hardly a success. The truth is I don't know who I am but a bride of Ethan Vertigo. I don't know what I'll do if I no longer serve people or be a dutiful wife."

Her guest did not smile but her face softened a little. The glow of fire engulfed the edges of her jaw, painting it orange and red, casting patches of amber between her knuckles. Memory was a cold thing, she came to understand, yawning like a hole in her head. It took more than it needed, remembered more than necessary, and molded itself on a whim.

"I am ashamed to admit this," she continued, almost choking on her tears, "but I had a more selfish intention than relieving your pain when I took you into this house. I was hoping... Perhaps, your presence would suffice to turn the tide. To help me repair my relationship with this town which, for some reason, refuses to accept my position."

Miss Karnstein listened to her in silence, her lips pressed together firmly, and Valerie thought she would storm out of the room and never come back. Tears threatened to fall again, her throat was closing with a stinging sensation, when Miss Karnstein left her seat and sat next to her. She leaned forward and stroked a strand of hair out of her face.

"My dearest Lady Valerie," whispered Miss Karnstein, her gaze lingering on the curve of her lips, "why must you burden yourself with such... unnecessary anxieties?"

Valerie traced her finger on the emerald stone. "But, Miss Karnstein, how can I not? The town deems me a wisp of a woman. What do I have to offer if not embroidery, insincere pleasantries, and year-long visits and parties?"

Miss Karnstein placed her hand over hers, the coldness of her touch chasing away the warmth of the fire. "I do not believe you're any more selfish than everyone else," she said, her voice a soft breeze on Valerie's nose. "Or think that you need to provide proof, give them a truth they cannot reject, to be worthy of love and respect. If that's what you wish, I'll help you, of course. But my darling, your merit does not reside in man-made accomplishments, nor worth in arbitrary pronouncements. You are not a creature to be tested or proven. I cherish you for who you are—a woman of kindness and compassion, and a heart that sings to me."

She put her hand over Valerie's heart. It thumped against her chill palm, taking on meaning, perhaps for the first time. Her voice was low and slightly husky. "Know that in my eyes, you will always be worthy and always loved."

Valerie was getting ready to sleep when she heard a knock on her door. She had been sitting in front of the fire for a while now, watching the flames curl around the logs and lick at the top of the hearth. She could not get Miss Karnstein's words out of her head and felt guilty for indulging in a fantasy of another life. She pondered what that would look like, yet all she saw was a dark void, yawning to swallow her whole.

"Come in," she said.

Miss Karnstein poked her head in. "I wanted to check how you were doing. You rather left the parlor in a hurry, Mrs. Vertigo." She was wringing her hands and biting her lip. "Have I hurt you?"

Valerie wiped a tear rolling down her cheek. "Oh gosh, no." She patted the cushion next to her. "Would you like to join me?"

After a long period of silence, Miss Karnstein nudged her elbow. "I've wanted to ask you this for a while. What would you like your life to be?"

"I don't know," she stammered, thinking about the void. She found herself awakened and agitated by the bluntness of the question. "I guess I've always believed someone else carved a place for me—even the slightest. I did not have to think about it before."

"Well, think now. There's nothing off limits. Anything you desire."

She became nervous. Her hands were shaking so she hid them under the cushion. There was a tingling in her spine, against her face; a stirring, white-hot thing. "I don't know," she repeated, "My mind fails to comprehend such a possibility."

"Let me help you then," Miss Karnstein said. "I'll go first." Her finger was idly tracing patterns on the worn rug. "I'm warm and from where I sit, I can see the moon. The night hums with the echoes of distant crowds. Promises, bargains, confessions. There's something else—someone. With me. I hear the heartbeat, as fast as mine, and it's so close. I want to cradle it, feel its mooring lines on my lips. Then I see the grieving face, perpetually perplexed, almost sinking, unreconciled, from my sight. I sit—It's a woman. I recognize the face. It's a face I'll never forget."

Valerie looked up, meeting Miss Karnstein's gaze. She smiled. "She holds my gaze and I smile. I want to look at her a little longer if she lets me. I want to know what she would do if I touched her."

Miss Karnstein reached out hesitantly, her fingers brushing against Valerie's cheek. The touch, light as a feather, sent a jolt of electricity through her chest. Miss Karnstein shifted on her cushion and leaned closer. The gaze of her intensity made Valerie's breath catch in her throat. Valerie wanted her fierceness to take over her, to remember the way her eyes flickered for the rest of her life. All meaning was forgotten between their hands: hers pressing lightly against her guest's cheek, Miss Karnstein's going up her waist.

The sight of her lingered, craving for more; the air crackled between them, charged with unnamed pleasures buried deep in her mind.

"What my heart screams," Valerie said, her voice barely a whisper, "my mouth cannot speak. It'll destroy us both."

Miss Karnstein's lips curled in a knowing smile. "Don't say it then. Just show me, Valerie."

A mouth opened next to hers, teeth flashing in the moonlight. Mircalla was next to her, lips parted, and Valerie had never felt this flesh of hers undulate this way before. She had been waiting for this moment and now it stood before her. She could almost taste it: sweet, dizzying, tender.

"Valerie," Mircalla breathed, her name a caress on Valerie's lips. "Say my name."

Valerie leaned in, her heart pounding a frantic rhythm against her ribs. "Mircalla," she whispered back, her voice thick with yearning she had been holding inside her. She would no longer deny it.

Their lips met and the world around them faded away, leaving only Mircalla's ravenous touch. Her lips ached with the taste of her. Her heart was a ricocheting bullet yet she was as calm as daybreak over the glistening snow. Nothing was lost; all was raw, bold, and unconditional. The swell of Mircalla's chest, the curve of her cracked lips, her trembling chin.

Mircalla held her tighter, their bodies crushing into one another, as she placed her lips on the crook of Valerie's neck first, then following the traces of her wound. Valerie moaned. She began to tremble, her head tilted back and her throat pulsing, as if she had been waiting for this moment.

"Oh, Mircalla." Valerie sighed, pulling away slightly, her eyes filled with wonder and trepidation. "If I could, I would tear this flesh apart and crawl into you."

Mircalla grinned and kissed her again, reaching out to cup her cheek, erasing every thought, flooding her mouth with a sense of escape that Valerie had never felt before. And tonight, she was bright and fearless, like a tear that would not hold stitches.

Valerie had been missing Mircalla like a pebble missed its bed at the bottom of the ocean, she was thus unmoving. It seemed trivial and mundane, but gave her a purpose, an imposing will to live. She must have changed. She felt it in her bones. Her heart was beating in her chest like a streaming river and she listened to its humming melody. It was steady, it was fast, and now, it was hers. She had longed to be seen, loved, and kissed, and she, for the first time, heard the sound of her heart as a song of devotion.

They could not stop laughing after Mircalla pulled back, giggling like schoolgirls racing to the carnation meadows. Valerie put her head on Mircalla's shoulder and she planted a kiss on the top of her head with a sigh. Her hand was drawing circles on Mircalla's back, as if to memorize the bumps and lines on her skin, and Mircalla, in turn, stroked her hair.

16

A SOFT HUSH PRESSED against the windowpanes. Valerie opened one eye, then the other, with Mircalla's hair woven through her fingers, blinking away the remnants of a dream. For days, there was only smoke rising, but today, the winter sun, muted by the swirling flakes, dappled the room in silver and gold.

On the other side of the bed, Mircalla nestled beneath the quilt. A gentle smile played on her lips, almost lost in the rise and fall of her breath. Valerie traced the curve of her chin with a phantom touch, her heart swelling with something closer to tenderness, gushing abundant from her fingertips. She listened to the muffled creak of the old house settling under the weight of winter. She knew she had angered the house, betrayed its legacy, yet she did not care.

Valerie got up and poked the fire and looked in the mirror. Was it a dream—a beautiful, irresistible dream—that intoxicated her and rendered her so miserable? She touched her neck, her heaving chest, searching for proof that she had really been kissed and held close. Was this the same pounding heart, the same trembling hand?

"Good morning, my lady," Mircalla murmured behind, eyes glinting in the pouring light.

"Do you fancy a walk?" Valerie asked, a mischievous edge in her voice. "I want to show you something."

Getting Mircalla to her room without Ethel seeing them proved to be a more difficult task than she had initially thought. Ethel was constantly moving from room to another—considering the state of the rooms, it was surprising—humming a tune to herself and going through the first chores of the day. They almost got caught when they were turning around to the hall where Mircalla's room was located. Ethel would have seen them if Valerie had not covered Mircalla's mouth and pulled her aside.

Once in the room, Valerie took a few breaths, trying to ignore the muffled sounds from the next room where Ethel was working. "Do not change into your dress yet," Valerie instructed Mircalla, grinning. "I have a surprise for you."

The next step was convincing Ethel to hand over the key to her husband's room. After that humiliating first night, they had never shared the same bed again, nor did they step into each other's room unless absolutely necessary. It felt strange to break this silent agreement between them.

As expected, Ethel was completely reluctant and against the idea. "But Madam," she screeched, "Sir Ethan does not even let me clean his own room! He requested me to carry the key unless he informs me beforehand."

The naked terror on her face annoyed Valerie. "Ethel, you're not listening! The doctor said he would get the clothes Mr. Vertigo wanted when the weather cleared. And it looks like the roads are clear today. I saw carriages passing by. I have to prepare Mr. Vertigo's belongings before the doctor arrives."

Ethel glanced around in guilt, as if Ethan could see her, and then handed her the key. It was a rusted, ornate thing that felt heavy in Valerie's hands. As soon as Ethel curtsied and took a few steps back, Valerie turned a corner and walked down the hallway, her skirt rustling behind.

When she stood in front of the door, she could smell whatever that was inside: pungent, sharp, like wet dogs. Valerie could not say anything about the room itself, for the heavy velvet curtains were drawn and the unused furniture was hidden under the sheets. She tripped over a bottle and almost fell, struggling to steady herself. The bed was not made and the crack of light from the hallway showed the piles of clothes, books, pens, and bottles of ink scattered everywhere. This was not a room of a gentleman, she thought, it was of a madman. On the far corner of the room stood another mahogany table. She had never made sense of why her husband kept a personal desk in every room, yet she could not help but take a peek. Crumpled papers, napkins, half-filled liquor bottles and empty glasses covered every visible surface. Drawers were left open.

Valerie found a stub of a candle amidst the blocks of sealing wax and lit it. The flickering flames revealed a more disastrous mess than she'd anticipate. Four pairs of trousers hung on his chair, wrinkled and the bottom hems folded, as if in a hurry. She tucked two pairs under her arm, covering her mouth, and turned to leave just before she saw a letter sitting on top of a shredded envelope. It had been folded and unfolded many times, yet the marks were clear and delicate, whatever this letter was had been handled with care. She would have walked away if this were another day, if she had not been pestered for months, if she had not recognized the name. Yet, there she was, rolling her tongue to say it. Emery Vertigo, it said in small, cursive letters. Another quick glance captured her husband's name and before the fragments of words cascaded in full sentences, Valerie grabbed the paper and slid it under the bodice of her dress.

"Madam, have you got what you need?"

Valerie hurried down the hallway and gave the key back, her heart thumping, her ears ringing. She stopped by her room before seeing Mircalla, thus anxious and shaken, and hid the letter under her mattress. She caught sight of herself in the cracked mirror, her cheeks flushed, a flimsy glaze over her eyes, very much like tears, yet she did not want to cry. On the contrary, when the rush of her deed faded away, a sense of calmness had come over her.

Mircalla was perched like a bird next to the tall window, watching the sun glistening over the peaks.

"Here I am!" Valerie announced herself, unable to hide the excitement in her voice. "My apologies, I didn't mean to keep you waiting."

"Oh, I've been wondering if you skipped town because you find me awfully boring!"

"Nonsense!" Valerie crossed the room and cupped Mircalla's face. "You are my best friend. I would never leave you behind."

"Such a relief," Mircalla giggled. "Well, where is the surprise?"

Valerie patted the trousers, still dangling over her arms. Mircalla's forehead creased with concern, eyes darting from the trousers to her, and a small frown curled her mouth in a rather unpleasant way.

"I'm not sure if I can really see it, darling. These look awfully like a man's trousers!"

"Well, yes! They are a man's trousers. But today, they are *our* trousers."

Mircalla tilted her head to the side as Valerie spoke. "I've been wanting to show you around the grounds of Vertigo Peaks and I thought a short walk can benefit us both. We have been confined within these walls for a while."

Mircalla looked out the window, sighing. "Don't you think it's too... bright outside?"

Valerie hummed. "The walk is quite short, my dear. We should be fine." She held Mircalla's hand. "Now, we must make haste before it gets dark and gloomy again! The trousers are quite odorous, if I may, but they should still fit us perfectly fine. My husband is not... quite colossal, you know."

"I hope you're not suggesting you find me fragile as a lily, Valerie. You're not a poet and I don't want to be a muse. That's a fickle, fleeting quality to possess, my dear." Mircalla wrapped her arms around her waist, her face close enough to see the purple veins on her nose. Valerie ached with the distant pain of Mircalla's sickness, shades of malady still lingering on those endearing features. Mircalla lay her head on her shoulder, a finger on her pulse, and they swayed in the room.

"I've never met anyone like you, Mircalla. I don't know what to think about you. I fear my heart might burst in its cage and I would still stand on my feet and look at you."

At this time of the year, the greenhouse was not as luscious and green. Nevertheless, Valerie wanted to show it to Mircalla. They did not talk much on their way. The chilling wind bit Valerie's cheeks while Mircalla walked glided past her with ease, as though the breeze made her float above the frozen ground. The trousers had proved to be practical and much to Valerie's surprise, liberating. Blood rushed to her head as she thought about the layers of her dress. Apparently, those were not made for mobility as Valerie felt her muscles tensing, her calves burning with vigor for the first time.

"Who are they?" Mircalla asked, pointing the way down the hills where a small group of people was watching them gingerly behind the high arched gate. Valerie winced at the sight of them. Mouths agape with wonder, they were pushing each other to press their heads between the rusted rods, pulling their horses closer to catch a better glimpse of her silhouette.

"I don't know them," Valerie responded. "Probably some folks from the town."

"Do they always watch you?"

Valerie followed her guest's widened eyes across the hills where people stood to survey their journey to the greenhouse, then stared off into space and pursed her lips. Yes, she wanted to admit, they were always watching her. Sneaking in from the forest or stalling by the gate, their looks were almost aimed at her, conjuring new ways to threaten and judge her serenity.

The steam from the greenhouse was visible even from the hills; it hung over the evening sky like a veil. Valerie desperately tried to fan the smoke out of her eyes as Mircalla pulled her in. Icicles hung like glittering fangs from the iron-wrought frame of the greenhouse. The door was unlocked and yielded with one push, swinging on its rusted hinges. It was brighter than she remembered. There were some old tools lying about, the dead leaves were caught in the eddies of the freezing wind. The plants the gardener had chosen for the season were thriving; their long leaves drooped like a cloak over the roof, luscious and warm, and every shade of green greeted them with lingering leisure.

She had always thought the greenhouse looked like her uncle's small cottage, uneven and left untended, but now as the lady drew her deeper, she realized how adorned and large the place was. They trailed along the cracked lines of various flowers and vegetables in silence, some plump, but most emptied.

"Do you like it?" Valerie asked. She let Mircalla wander around the place, amazed and filled with giddy excitement, and found a secluded corner for herself, shaded enough to rest, with a clear view of her guest who was pacing the rows of plants, and unlike Valerie, already oblivious to the people outside the gate.

She took off her shawl and rubbed her temples. The greenhouse was very warm and damp, the slant of winter sun so bright that steam billowed up. Valerie loosened her collar and unbuttoned the first two buttons of her chemise, her throat was throbbing with thirst. She raised a hand, slick with sweat, and pushed the loose strands of her hair away from her face. She closed her eyes to rest but all she saw was the people behind the gate, peering in with their long heads, twisting their wobbly necks like reptiles.

"This is a heavenly place." Mircalla's voice was distant yet Valerie heard the ringing laughter in her voice; she chimed like a bell that finally found its rhythm and sang its own song. Valerie replied wearily. "Indeed."

"What's wrong?"

Valerie heard the ruffle of her skirt first, then cracked an eye open and saw Mircalla's troubled face hovering above her. Sunlight was cascading behind her, among the orchids, and made a halo over her head, making her look like one of those heavenly creatures from old paintings. Wings spread for flight, silk draped around her figure. She sat next to her, sliding a finger over a strand of stray hair and tucking it behind her ear. "Why are you sulking?"

Valerie was parched and voiceless. All flustered and in the clasp of tremors and unease. She regretted leaving the house. She did not like being exposed like a cut on the cheek, anticipating a sea of faces following her with vile words in their mouths.

"Will you not speak?"

"Let's go back," Valerie said with a high voice. "I'm rather tired."

"It's about the people, is it not?" Mircalla let out an exasperated sigh. "The more you give, the more they take. You know they will. Why do you torment yourself with these fading things? For they shall wilt." She crushed a leaf with the sole of her boot and fixed her gaze on Valerie. In this tempestuous humor of hers, she did not like her guest. She had a contemptuous look about her that made Valerie agitated, mingled with a sense of aberration and fear. Her face well-lit under the sun, the whites of her eyes almost invisible, Mircalla looked like a vast and terrifying scene, like standing at the end of a precipice.

"This is not some sort of a fancy party or a private ladies' club that I can walk out of. This is...what they expect of me. The town, my husband...I vowed to be here. I cannot turn my back to them."

"And what do you expect of yourself? Are you going to spend the rest of your days here, living with what-ifs? Will it matter then?"

"Yes!" Valerie jumped to her feet, tears welling in her eyes. "Maybe. It matters now and that's all I can allow myself to think about. What is left of me if I reject the love of duty, that devotion to clarity, that makes affairs bearable, makes inevitable comforting? All I have, I owe it to him, his house, and his name. It's not easy, Mircalla. It's not easy. Please do not confuse me when it's clear that you have not been in a similar position."

Mircalla's upper lip trembled, and a stifled cry broke from her throat.

"I have endured hardships and sorrow the likes of which you've yet to witness, Mrs. Vertigo."

"How could I know? This discreet, stilted attitude leaves much to imagination." Valerie breathed heavily in the still. "I don't know you."

"There's no need for a quarrel, my dear. If what I relinquished to you amounts to nothing, I'll leave. I asked for your discretion. I'll dare and ask for more—I want you to wait. I shall reveal everything when it's time but I beg you, please do not attack me on the matter."

Mircalla stood as if she were on the verge of tears as her face transformed once. She shook her head, admitting defeat, and knelt before her and said in a muffled voice, "Will you not accept me? Will you not take me as your own?"

"Mircalla," Valerie gasped. Snow started to swirl around them again. It was getting dark. "Let's go back."

But Mircalla was stubborn. "Tell me this is not what you want," she said, her lips brushing Valerie's ear. "Tell me you're not ravished with the same burning ache in your heart and I'll walk away." She reached out, her touch sending a ripple through the air, and caressed the back of her neck.

"Mircalla...I can't..."

Hurt crept upon Mircalla's face and she stared at the plants, scowling. Valerie wanted to say more, but another voice echoed behind them.

"Mrs. Vertigo? Is that you, madam?"

Valerie retreated a few steps back and stood as far from Mircalla as possible. She coughed into her palm, trying to keep her voice steady. "Yes, Mr. Faulkner. It's me."

The old Mr. Faulkner appeared behind the orchids. He was holding a garden trowel in one hand, a half-eaten cabbage in the other.

"Are you alright, madam? Are you sick?" He paused, his face closer than she'd like, and pointed a gnarled finger at her. "I can fetch Ethel if you like."

Valerie looked at his weathered face, covered in freckles, as though someone scattered a handful of seeds. His cap was hanging from his belt, his sleeves were rolled up. Although his voice bore no sign of anger, Valerie could see that he wished her gone. Even the tip of his grayish mustache was vibrating with worry.

A faint smile passed her lips. "No, thank you. We were just leaving."

Mircalla stood up next to her, ostensibly busying herself with brushing dead leaves from her coat and the man's face changed. It took on a horrid ashen pallor. Before he did not seem to breathe, but now his chest rose and fell in small bursts and Valerie noticed his eyes turning red. He gulped and gasped like a fish stranded on sand, but in minutes, these shades faded and he gave them a curt nod before walking off, mumbling something, but Valerie heard what he said: "The crops are dying in town, and soon, the decay will reach here to its heart. This house is a sinkhole; it will suck us all in."

Valerie rushed to the front of the greenhouse, the trousers swirling around her boots, the air escaping from her lungs all at once, before Mircalla could catch up with her.

17

VALERIE DID NOT SLEEP that night. What was she thinking? Mircalla Karnstein was a mere guest she had saved from a snowstorm. She could not understand her mercurial twists of temper, the way she disappeared in the morning hours, and why she kept Valerie in the dark about the reason she was here and where she intended to go. Valerie was a married woman, the mistress of Vertigo Peaks for that matter, and this brazen and secret intimacy would ruin them both. The rawness of the feeling would not shelter them forever. She would be Mrs. Vertigo, even if she were stranded in this town, living in the credence of seclusion.

Sometimes, in those rare minutes that shattered her perception, she was convinced that it was she that never existed. She had been merely hurled into this room. She was born in this room, crawled in this room, grew up and bled in this room, and God cut her web of fate with an indifference that grew larger every day.

But even as Mircalla headed to the woods, her white nightgown billowing white against the night, somehow, Valerie could only picture her lips brushing hers, her soft caress etched on her skin, making her heart jump and skin blush with anticipation for more. She shook her head and drew the curtains. They were two souls caught up in the thrill of the moment, such an act would never be repeated again. It didn't matter what she wanted. She had already made her choice. The aching would be forgotten, the shards of her heart would mend, but betrayal would never.

The next day, she found herself in the greenhouse again. The moonlight streamed through the windows as she sat on the same bench, her head in her hands, rocking back and forth. She had not caught a glimpse of Mircalla since yesterday after she disappeared in the forest and she remained indifferent to Ethel's knocks on her door. There was no word from her husband or the doctor and Valerie spent the day alone, wishing to wail in agony, yet her limbs were stiff. She knew she had not wandered off her path, that she was true to her vow, but in the deepest corners of her soul, there arose the pang, even in the back of her eyes, of envy and longing, coursing through her like an icy river.

A clicking sound, the snow crunching, distant sobbing sounds. Valerie hid behind a barrel, frantically searching for something she might use to protect herself from this intruder, and pressed a hand over her mouth to not scream. Was it someone from the town, furious yet again, and ready to attack? She tried to catch a glimpse of the person. It sounded like a woman's voice, mingling with the whir of the wind, sobbing for breath. Valerie found an empty can of paint. The intruder was moving closer, tripping on the gravel, and still crying, and thus Valerie raised the can and threw herself in front of the stranger with a cry.

It was Mircalla. But it was not who she had met at that party. The bright, altogether blithesome, and spiritless, heavenly creature was gone. This was a phantom, a restless apparition, shoulders jerking with each motion, wailing into the cold night. She did not even give a start when Valerie faced her, only removed one hand from her face and Valerie thought about all the stone angels she had seen in mossy churchyards. She had not noticed the crimson of her hands, her gown, her stomach before. Hunched over her knees, her eyes opaque, she seemed to shrink into herself, the outline of her body wavering under the pale moon.

"Mircalla..." Valerie's voice sounded strange to herself, weak and hoarse. "What happened?" She could not look at her face, for there was so much crimson that it burned her eyes. Near the door where she stood was slick with that hue, a small pool reflecting her limp figure.

Mircalla's eyes widened, but she didn't say anything. Valerie saw the sadness and confusion flit across her face, and she drew back against the iron-wrought door, effacing herself before Valerie could reach out. She was a bolt of lightning one could only see through the corner of their eyes and if she didn't look at her close enough, she might miss her, just like she was now. Valerie crossed the aisles of plants with heavy footsteps, overcome with fear, trying not to look at the trail of blood, and took Mircalla's hand.

"Tell me," Valerie insisted. "Are you hurt?" At the same time, she was checking if her guest was injured. The vacant look on her face had dissipated yet she was still gasping for breath.

"I...I don't..." Mircalla replied, stammering to a halt. She gave her hand a squeeze and Mircalla looked at her unknowingly, her lip trembling. It was a sad sight that brought tears to Valerie's eyes, like standing in front of a burning house. There was no one else lingering outside, only the constant tap of melting snow from the roofs. Tap, tap, tap. Valerie carried Mircalla to the bench.

Valerie watched her breathing slow down, her shoulders relax, her lips form again. The creases around her eyes disappeared, the knowing glimmer returned to her eye, and the quiver of her brow smoothed. Her own hands were covered in blood and she had this intense desire to wash it off. Yet, Valerie had not expected to find the rustling, the undulating of her nightgown, every time Mircalla's chest rose and fell, so peaceful. The sheer lack of absoluteness in her temperament was engaging, more than she was willing to admit. She scratched her neck, brushing the faint swell of her wound.

"I don't remember," Mircalla breathed out, swaying a little, lost in her own thoughts. "I was running in the forest. Then I heard a voice, thinking it was you, I ran after it. But I don't remember..." She went quiet for a moment, then squinted, as though she was seeing Valerie for the first time. "If I am a little bit ill at ease, it is because I am without resolution, without strength."

She pressed Valerie in a tight embrace, murmuring soft words into her ear, her lips trailing down her cheeks, and although Valerie wished to tear herself apart from this frenzied encounter, her body failed her. All her emotional properties slipped in the same trace that she had felt when that woman lured her into the forest and bit her on that sinister night.

"Come with me. To the woods, to a dark alley, away from this rotting house. It's maddening to watch you from afar, hear your breath but not feel your beating heart. I've never chosen a thing before, and here I am, bewildered and out of mind, choosing you."

She placed her hands about Valerie's neck, and drew her nearer. A shiver ran through her spine, not from the cold, but from Mircalla's gaze that burned into her back. Then, with the deliberate tenderness of a predator claiming its prey, Mircalla's mouth found hers.

Her lips were cold and hungry. They parted slightly and Valerie, her body awakened by the familiar intimacy, slipped her tongue inside. It was intense, so intense that she felt irrevocably lost and sore in the bitter January winds. This time was different. The movement of their lips was imbued with a sense of imminence. It was rough and waxy, as if peeling layers of tissues from her skin, unraveling all the muscles and veins and nerves. Valerie sank on Mircalla's shoulder, throwing her head back. The last thing she remembered was the alarming closeness of her guest, her chest crushing against hers; one hand laced with her undone hair, the other fumbling to take off her chemise. A lethargy settled on her; part desire, part aching.

Mircalla pushed her against the bench, one thigh tentatively between her legs, the soft tickle of her breath under her nose. The metallic, biting smell of blood filled Valerie's lungs as they struggled to be closer. Mircalla stooped over and kissed her breast over the tight corset, only her eyes visible, and when she raised her head, Valerie saw the dark red on her skin where Mircalla's mouth left its mark. One of Mircalla's hands moved down slowly, circling around her stomach, and found the buttons of her trousers, then her lips followed, leaning the side of her face against the loose cloth. Her body was convulsing, straining, pinned to the bench, the cold metal digging into her back. She tried to move her arms around, her body a feverish lump, and a deep sigh escaped from her lips.

"Please stop," Valerie whispered into the night and the woman drew herself back, leaving a soreness and an unbearable headache in her wake, "We cannot do this. Not tonight."

Without the shape of Mircalla's body, her own felt like an empty sack. She bent her limbs, drawing up to her stomach, and tried to button her chemise with unsteady hands. Blood had dried under her nails. Mircalla stirred, puckering her lips and fluttering her lashes, as though she was roused from her reverie. She sat stiffly beside her, her gaze flitting across the moonlit panes. The silence stretched between them, the only sound the dripping water from the roof.

"What is it?" Mircalla asked, sour-toned and strident, as she grew more languid and ill-tempered. Her hand was hovering in the air, inches from Valerie's cheek.

"Who are you, Mircalla? Why can't you confide in me when you confess how you love me? Why can't you tell me the truth? Is it-is it because you fear I'll banish you?"

"Valerie…"

"I don't know who I am when you touch me and talk to me so. It rips my very being apart. You tell me I'm foolish for wanting the respect of the townspeople, yet I see no other path than this."

"You cannot trade one curse with another, my dear Valerie."

"I know. But if a part of you remains hidden, locked away from me, how can I surrender to your touch? How can I know if I am not running into the arms of another curse? One that is calamitous and insurmountable, for it pierces through my heart with love and lightness?" Valerie choked out, her voice trembling. "What else can I call you but a spark, a beam of light? That's what you are to me. That's when you come to me, in the darkest hour of my night. Yet, I cannot bring myself to lay bare in front of you, witnessing your surreptitious meetings and covert myths about yourself. I cannot help but feel that I am a target of treachery. Tell me, are you here to wreck my home and add your own mockery to my name?" asked Valerie through gritted teeth, gripping Mircalla's shoulders. "This is precisely what I have been running away from, what I have been punished with. So, no. I will not trade one curse with another Mircalla. I will not bear another persecution."

Valerie pressed her palms to her eyes, almost sobbing. "Valerie, my darling. Come here," Mircalla said, her voice devoid of vehemence or the overpowering ardor, merely a hollow echo, irritated by the inconvenience of the moment. Then her voice gained strength, her breath gracing her forehead. She planted a kiss between her fingers and moved Valerie's hands from her face.

"You bring me joy beyond measure," Mircalla told her, in a voice as soft as a murmur. "My heart is wounded when you're not near. I close my eyes to whisper your name—yes, call me a heathen—for I cannot see past the world without your welcoming arms. And it pains me to see you believe I'd ever betray you when I just love you so. I'll show you what I have endured and risk my heart being broken." She kissed the top of her head. "Tomorrow, we shall meet again."

18

CRIMSON FOG SWIRLED, OBSCURING the edges of her bed; shadows twisted on the floorboards. A chill seeped through the shredded tapestries, despite the roaring fire in the hearth across the room. Was it the firelight flickering or the charred remnants of her sanity slipping away? A hand, frigid and solid like a glacial lake, grasped hers, and untethered Valerie from the world like a great galleon, weathered yet sailing its voyage back home. The dampness spread from her burning forehead to her collarbones. She shivered, her clammy skin prickling as the fever tightened its grip. Through a coat of sweat, she glimpsed visions. A voice, familiar yet unraveling, murmured lullabies as she slept. She was there, she knew, somewhere in the dark corners of the room. Just out of reach, beyond the tendrils of rescue.

Valerie straightened to hear the voice, to feel the touch once more. Was that her laugh, echoing from the frosted panes, or was it a scream? Her heart hammered against her ribs and she was fading in and out of consciousness. Then, a flicker of movement at the doorway. A tall figure silhouetted against the flames, casting a shadow that stretched across her quilts. The flimsy boundary between dream and reality shifted, broke away from its lull and oblivion.

"Mircalla?" Valerie croaked, her voice a dry rasp.

The silhouette stepped closer, the firelight bathing the face in a warm, amber glow. In the liminal space between dreams and wakefulness, she saw her face, etched with compassion and worry, imposed on the fog that still swirled around her grotesquely. Mircalla appeared behind the fog, holding her hand, the furrow between her brows casting dark shadows over her countenance.

"My love," Mircalla replied and Valerie felt her cheeks get wet, as though she was walking in the morning mist, but she did not know if she was crying. Mircalla settled onto the edge of the bed, the worn wooden frame groaning under her weight. She cradled Valerie's hand in her own and the reeling world stopped for a moment. The blurred edges came into focus.

"You have been so sick, Valerie. But I'm here."

"What happened? I can't—" Valerie tried to sit upright, but Mircalla laid her down again, putting her head on the pillows. "Do not strain yourself, my dear. You're still too weak." She breathed deeply and sniffled. Was she crying? In her hand, Mircalla held a steaming cup, the scent of tea and lemon aroused her spirits. Valerie did not protest when Mircalla held the teacup to her lips. She took small sips, the sweet and sour taste soothing her parched throat. The silence in the room was only broken by her hoarse breathing and the crackling fire. She thought she was waiting for something to happen, the sudden releases of breath billowing out between them. Yet, in Mircalla's company, Valerie did not want to untangle the world or face a revelation. She lapsed into another reverie that lasted until her guest spoke again.

"Valerie, I must tell you—" Mircalla said, but before she could finish her sentence, the doctor and Ethan barged in, loudly discussing something Valerie could not figure out. Mircalla jumped to her feet, wiping her eyes quickly with the back of her hands, and gave a curt bow to the gentlemen.

"I am certain it is the flu or fatigue!"

"She took to her bed with fever and frenzy, my friend. We have to evaluate every possibility."

"Valerie," Ethan gasped, his head low. The doctor was already by her side, rummaging through his bag of bottles and herbs and peculiar liquids. His vials clinked as he regarded her with Valerie thought to be pity. The glisten of perspiration on his upper lip, his tightened jaw, the vein pulsing on his temple lurched her stomach. He sat where Mircalla was sitting a moment ago. Where did she go?

Mircalla stroked her hair and said with a faint smile before leaving the room, "I haven't forgotten about my promise. You rest well, my dear. I'll come and see you later."

"Now... let's see what we have here. How do you do, Mrs. Vertigo?" He took her pulse. "We have been very worried about your health."

Valerie did not wish to speak. She could feel her husband's eyes on her, intent and solemn, but did not look up. "May I?" The doctor pointed at her chest. Valerie nodded. He loosened her nightgown to place a cold metal device on her heart, and pulled a glass thermometer and placed it in her mouth. Suddenly, Valerie was conscious of her body as one might be conscious of it in a free fall, seconds before a crush, a horripilation of dread tingling down the skull, warming the spine. Once everything was set, the physician cast a furtive glance at his friend, his nostrils flared, and whispered to Valerie, "I'm sorry to ask you this, madam, but is there any chance I can see your neck?"

Ethan was chewing on his lip, swaying on the heels of his boot, then said in a rather high voice, "I'll be back in a minute. Please carry on."

"Madam?"

The scorching, searing, freezing pain of her wound made Valerie wince. She knew what the doctor was looking for, what the outcome would be. Her heart almost catapulted out of her chest, but she was too consumed by fever to resist. The doctor braced her chin, tracing the jawline then turned her head to the side, exposing the throbbing neck. Valerie did not have to see her wound to know what it looked like: It was the mark of the plague.

The doctor grunted. "Mrs. Vertigo... Why haven't you sent someone for me? Why did you hide it? Why?"

What could she say? Throwing herself into the belly of the disease seemed more tolerable than the judgment and isolation that the plague brought. Even if she confessed that it was a woman pacing in the woods, staring and piercing her soul with scarlet eyes, the doctor would not believe her.

"My lady, you know... Recovery..."

Valerie replied, her breaths growing shallow and quick. "Yes, I am aware."

He stood up, turning a vial in his hand before squirting the milk white substance on a handkerchief covered in dark brown spots, and without warning, pressed it on her neck. Valerie dug her nails into her palms to not scream as he tore a crust of scab with the cloth.

"You are angry at me," exhaled Valerie. The scowl on his face made him look scarier, and Valerie realized, he was fighting tears back. He cleaned the wound with cotton and brought bandages, and without looking at her once, said, "We must leave speculations aside and focus on your recovery, madam."

"But you are."

"Well... That goes without saying, madam."

"I'm sorry, doctor."

"The damage is done, madam. There's no need for an apology.

After two weeks of various treatments, Valerie was able to move around her room without assistance. She was confined to her bed for most days, battling with fever and lesions of pus, however, she was never left alone. It eventually got so annoying to the point that Valerie locked herself in the room. The constant vigilance, inspection of her wound, burning incense with the hopes of eradicating the disease, or being the subject of unconventional medicine experiments had further devastated her nerves. She was getting better and it made the doctor curious and suspicious in equal measure. A palpable change was hanging in the air, yet Valerie was uninterested and reluctant about its circumstances. It was easier and much preferable to sit by the window, contemplate about the horrors of her illness, and resort to the meandering ways of her mind. The issues and complexities of life had become overbearing. She wanted to be left unobserved, like a distant star which was nothing but a cloud of dust and light, yet by no coincidence, she was pulled back to the realm of mystery and secrets once more.

It was the same day Mircalla returned. Valerie had not seen her after she left the room with the same promise, punctuated with a hearty voice and well wishes, and now she was lingering at the doorway, staring at her, the curling flames reflecting her gaze.

"You look better."

Valerie did not reply. Instead, she gave her a half-smile and turned to watch the snow-covered peaks, the pine trees looming in the back, from her frosted window. Her sagging cheeks hurt with the motion but she managed to keep her posture erect. She could not bring herself to look at this outlandish woman without a swelling bitterness in her mouth. Their intimate moments seemed so distant now, as if they belonged to someone else, that Valerie believed she only inherited its account from another person and mythologized them. It dawned upon her, with the lights of sadness traversing her body, that she was left behind like a holy relic no one wished to possess anymore. But, she was no saint or martyr. She had to cope.

"Are you vexed with me?" Mircalla leaned in to see her face. "Will you not speak?"

Dust motes had stirred up, swimming in the room. While everybody was busy examining Valerie, nobody had paid attention to the damp sheets, piles of ashes in the hearth, and pieces of cloth lying around on the floor with scabs from her wounds.

"Don't hide from me, Valerie."

"What?" Valerie glared at her. "What is there for me to say that you already don't know?"

Valerie saw her nodding in the corner of her eye, giving her thoughts a new turn. The brooding intensity with which Mircalla looked at her was disturbing.

"I know what it feels like to be trapped. The constant humiliation, being the first person everyone looks at when something goes awry, fearing if you'll survive another day when there is a dizzying, permanent longing inside you that wants to dig the roots of the earth to make a bed for yourself, and when you find a place, a person, that covered in the saps of creation, who is evergreen despite everything, you don't let them go. You hold the pressure in your hands and whisper sweet nothings to it. You make another bed." Mircalla held her hand, gently pressing her thumb on her colorless knuckles. "You move me, carry me to a place beyond recognition. What an embarrassment—how foolish I am to hurt you. I'm sorry, Valerie. You're much dearer to me than a friend and I-I am put to grieve when you look so! Let us put this behind and never waste a moment again. I made a promise to you and I intend to keep it. I'll tell you who I really am. Come with me tonight, darling."

Valerie laughed between hot tears. "You'd be a terrific poet, but I know to never ask for a rose garden."

Mircalla had her head down, trying to hide her smirk. "That, I'll never promise. Will you run away with me tonight?"

19

A FLURRY OF SNOW met them at the gates. The Vertigo Peaks stood on its solitary hills, proud and piercing the sky, but Valerie felt its ferocious vibrations like crashing waves. It looked like a wasteland with its many windows shone under a sunken glaze, stretching in all directions, neglected and shaking to its foundations. She felt someone or something watching her, the cold breath on her back, but they entered the forest undisturbed, hand in hand, running like schoolgirls.

It was a steep road with trees extended in every direction. Valerie and Mircalla were dancing, their ridiculous hats hardly on their heads in the wind, boots crunching on the untouched snow, reminding them that they were the first to wander, stretching before their eyes like a blanket and Valerie had a prodigious appetite for crushing every little dead branch and shouting over the midnight birds. It was a perverse sensation too, for there was vindication and voyeurism at surveying this little corner of the earth, as if they possessed and bent it to their will, and conquering it with their steps.

Her knees were trembling with exercise and looking over at Mircalla, Valerie noticed the deep languor on her face was smoothing away.

"Where to?" she screamed, her hair blowing in the wind. A murder of crows took flight, flapping about them with a discordant squawk. Mircalla looked at her triumphantly but did not speak. Thatched roofs emerged behind the trees, the smell of coal against the bitter chill of the night was mixed with the thick, oily fog. A sizzling-hot lump formed in the back of her throat. It hurt her to look at this vastness, this light. Only to see vengeance and animosity. She knew these houses stored storms and fury while their candles burned with fondness for anyone but her. She had never been worthy of their affection.

Yet, she was more disappointed in herself to have tried to capture their hearts. She had let them put her on display like a caged animal presented for entertainment. No, she should have known, from the very first day, when they lay their calloused hands upon her, that she would turn to spite and injury for consolation, for preservation of her mind.

The town had taken a new form with heavy falls of snow. It had retreated, shrunk into itself while the glistening frost bit at Valerie's knuckles. She huddled deeper into her cloak, her breath billowing like smoke in the frigid air while her teeth were chattering against the roof of her mouth. The thrill in the forest had vanished. What were they doing? Two ladies high in rank in trousers, dashing around breathless like mischievous children, pretending to be free, fanciful in their ambitions. An enigmatic guest and her bashful host.

"Are you sure you want to do this...whatever is it that you want to do?"

Valerie stopped with a jolt, her hand hanging between them. Mircalla took it and kissed her palm. "Are you afraid?"

"I am only ever mindful of grander obligations and my failures."

"When I look at you, I am only reminded of how I would risk everything to lay beside you so you may never go cold. And I know, you would do the same. Whisper to your little heart, my dear Valerie, to shed its sorrow and those parts that keep you away from me."

Mircalla touched her arm and tucked a strand of hair behind her ear. Valerie met her gaze and she saw not just a promise, but a reflection of something deeper—hunger awaiting her, hunger searching for her, hunger she already gratified. The doubts, the fears, they receded, replaced by a fierce determination. Taking a deep breath, Valerie reached out, and took her face in her hands.

Despite the complete stillness of her body, her mind was unquiet. But it did not change the fact that Mircalla saw her, who she really wanted to be, and in her heart of hearts, Valerie knew she would be held together by the gravity of this happenstance.

If, she thought, this woman found her in the desert and begged for a drop of rain, she would cut herself in half and let her blood run like a river. If she needed a voice to sing, she would cut her tongue and make herself speechless. She would make herself a god and an abomination to hold this feeling a little longer. This sweet obsession, the tantalizing promise of recognition was enough to rekindle Valerie's faith. If her perseverance was the result of someone's privation, then so be it, she thought.

"I've never been to this part of the town before!"

Mircalla was leading the way ten steps ahead, her limbs waving like a flag, the thin air of midnight meandering gently around the outline of her body, and they ducked into a small alley where a few women laughed like hyenas and coughed like drunkards next to a stack of wooden boards, shutters of bedrooms half open like dim eyes. She plowed her way through the deep snow, the raw dirt and smell of urine clinging to her clothes, while Mircalla sauntered on, slowly, the back of her neck tucked neatly in her collar. The place was a maze. She would have got lost if it weren't for Mircalla's head bobbing around. Valerie wondered how many times she had been here before, stepping in and out of the narrow streets, outstretching her arms, inhaling the sharp smell of liquor and grease.

"Where are we going?" Valerie asked.

"I thought we might stop for a drink before we head to the last stop on our route."

She winked and pulled Valerie into a small pub. Men were swarming to its vicinity, slurring their speech and crying tears of laughter, while women rubbed their backs on the walls, their braids caught in the chilling air. A warm light spilled from the pub's windows, a cacophony of voices singing over the appalling tune. They walked past the crowd, pretending to be gentlemen, inattentive to the teary eyes and inquiring whispers. The clink of beer mugs infested the room; men gathered in corners discussing nothing in particular made Valerie increase the pressure on Mircalla's arm. The floor was sticky with spilled beer and gin, long trails along the polished woods. Clamorous, overexcited voices rose from every table, people treading the place with an unseen energy, their tittle-tattle louder than the music. One man caught Valerie's attention as he banged his fist on the table while the other two belched in his face with their toothless smiles. It was the first time Valerie saw them, not in the background of her life, but in bursts on her peripheral vision; neither droopy nor exhausted from the day's work, not a crack of exertion on their wet mouths, not pinched or wretched. Their eyes were not narrowed with spite, and the tongues did not curl in disgust with her name. When she was absent from their lives, they were normal people with reddish streaks running through their drunk faces, lips eaten in guilt, drinking beer at midnight.

Valerie shook off the snow from the folds of her cloak after Mircalla gestured to the bar. "I'll get us two beers," she yelled and disappeared into the crowd. She kept her head low, rapping her fingers on the table and humming to the tune. Nobody seemed to notice them, the chatter went on, beers got lukewarm, the dancing feet grew tired but kept on dancing. Mircalla sat across from her and pushed a heavy mug of beer. She fingered the thin rim of the glass slowly while Mircalla was looking at her intently, the sparks in her eyes reflecting the pub's yellow light but Valerie knew something darker was lurking beneath.

"Have you ever wanted to choose another name? To be someone else, untethered from all that came before you, and entirely bound to yourself alone? To outrun yourself?"

Valerie took a sip of her cold beer and licked her lips. The warmth spread from her throat to her stomach, the bitter taste sliding down her tongue like an ice cube, the sweat on the glass cooling her hot fingers as her vision doubled. "I've been taught to embrace it like a ghost who only loves the house it haunts. It is interesting, you know, what a name does to your body."

"What does it do?"

Valerie chuckled. "It decays mine, I'm afraid. Yet, I've never seen someone whose body grows luxuriantly when their name passes the lips."

"Is it a curse, you think?"

Her snort of laughter came to a halt. Mircalla had found a half-eaten raw potato and rolled it across the loose boards. A shade of scarlet flashed across her face. Valerie rubbed her eyes. "What do you know about the curse?" she asked, suddenly alert and somber.

Mircalla looked weary and old. Hunching her shoulders against the men, the music, the quarrels. Her eyes dimmed, slanted with a darkness so persistent that bred hopelessness. Valerie swallowed hard.

"I can't quite remember it except for a few fragments here and there," she shrugged, "but maybe this is better." She gulped the rest of her beer. "What I know is, however, that it rattles you. And the worst of all, in one blink, it will ruin you. I feel it when you quicken your pace, when you bury your cheek to your cloak, when you walk past the long halls of your home. Vertigo Peaks is not fit to protect you." She drew in a sharp breath. "It will all fall down but not before I will burn their hearts first."

"How do you know all of this? Who told you?"

"Let's not shift our attention from one secret to another, dear." Mircalla reached over the table and pressed her hand with a bewildered look; her eyes darted up and down, her gaze piercing past her neck. "But this itch... I had it once." She got up and fastened her cloak. The cloud of fury passed from her face; her countenance expressed forbearing. "Come. We have a place to be."

As they wandered the dark streets, everything appeared in a state of disentanglement from the mind's tenacious hold, far out of reach, and bathed in the friendly charm of snow, bordering. Valerie felt her heart lighten, taking a new shape under the layers of clothing, her feet did not flounder as it used to do and Mircalla was by her side. She pulled Valerie to a corner and pushed her against the wall. Her hand scraped the cold stone. They were breathing heavily into each other's faces, sending clouds of vapor into thin air, and Mircalla's pupils were so large that Valerie saw herself in them. There was a pause, a silent agreement, signed in the eyes and carried by the lips. Mircalla pressed a hand to the nape of Valerie's neck and pulled her closer. The distance seemed insurmountable, yet there she was, reminded of her heart.

When her lips moved, Valerie moved as well, impatient. "I want to taste you," Mircalla said. Valerie's mouth was dry; she grew weary of words. Instead, she nodded. Mircalla got rid of the hat and stroked her tousled hair, let the dark curls sway in the wind, then fixed her stare, as if drinking the moment. Knowing her, Valerie hoped it would be quick but when Mircalla's hand slipped through her shirt, pressing the nail of her thumb against her chin, she could not help but let out a trembling sigh. Her pulse edged in the back of her thighs.

"Open your mouth," Mircalla grinned, leaning closer.

No hunger was ever this satisfied; Valerie wanted to hold her and invite her deeper, inside, where every fiber of her existence exploded with one name. She shifted a little to run her fingers through Mircalla's long silver-dusted hair but she pinned Valerie's hands above her head, still with that wicked grin. The cold stones were hard against her back while Mircalla was all soft like a daydream, rocking her back and forth.

Valerie was not taught to think that the touch of lips could end the world, but as she stood breast to breast with Mircalla, she knew the desire would consume her and scrape her flesh off the bone.

The bare longing right between her legs where Mircalla cradled herself was enough to hurl herself into a half-forgotten life, she moaned and threw her head back, as if she was nothing but a soft clump of bones.

"Please," she gasped for air. But Mircalla was a cruel lover. She kissed her eyes first, then the tip of her nose, and only then followed her lips the path of her cold hands, sliding down the neck. Valerie wriggled, restless and wanting, until Mircalla came back to her lips. She tasted like cheap beer and Valerie had never wanted to laugh more. However, Mircalla silenced her as her tongue made its way in her mouth; a promise of sin and salvation.

She dared to think of her husband once, but the image vanished quickly as Mircalla bit her lower lip, teeth sunk deep into that rose shape, and Valerie felt the warmth of her own blood fill her mouth. She moaned when Mircalla pulled back, then saw her mouth smeared with her blood, as if she had just eaten wild berries, and watched it trickle down to her chin.

A sound of footfalls came first, then the vulgar tongues rose. Valerie craned her neck and got a glimpse of a small group of drunkards, gathering like a pack of wolves at the end of the street.

"Oi, you ratbags! What you're doing here, coddling each other?"

Valerie could not believe she was not dreaming a frightful nightmare; she was wakeful and staring at the men, yet Mircalla, still gazing dreamily at her lips, ignored their renewed titter and snort.

"Come on now, dandy! Lost your way? I sure know where you can go. Your mom's loving arms." He drummed his hands on his knees, laughing. "You can come into mine too."

"Gentlemen," Mircalla greeted them from afar. Valerie hoped they did not hear the feminine tinge in her voice. "I'm afraid you're at the wrong party. What's the matter?"

"Having a tad conversation with you lot, eh? What are you doing at this time of night? Wait a second." He stepped back and likewise, other men retreated on cue. It was very theatrical. "Are you one of the creditors?" His face soured under moonlight, a puff of smoke from his cigarette blowing out of the corner of his mouth. A gleam caught in his eye, pensive and suddenly taciturn and the group fell silent for a moment.

"That I am not."

"Good." The man grinned. Cheers and roars rang in the air. "That chap left the cottage and won't return."

"Is that so?" Mircalla started walking towards them, a hand in her pocket, her voice dangerously low. "If I ring the bell and ask for a good-for-nothing son or a husband, will they tell me the man left?" She clicked her tongue. "Or will I find a screaming babe in the arms of a wailing mother, accursing the man for drinking too much and never bringing bread to his house?"

"You vazey fucking..." he spat contemptuously as the bottle in his hands shattered on the snow and the fists rose in its place. The other men imitated him as well, babbling about Mircalla being an unfair fellow, provoking them to start a fight, and that they would show it to her what it meant to fall on her ass. Their mouths were gaps, drooling and toothless like old men. That's when Valerie noticed the lines on their faces, the crack in their voices, their grizzly beards. Although strands of black and brown showed about their ears and their thick brows, they stood listless, withdrawing themselves, like condemned men. They could not have been older than her husband, yet they did not stir but only gaped at her wide-eyed.

"Let's go," Valerie whispered to Mircalla, who was striding towards the group. The curdling inside her kept her from moving.

The sound of laughter again. A flash of sharp teeth in the shadows. It was Mircalla. "But if you keep annoying me, I'll make sure you never speak again. It would be hard to beg when you're tongueless, right?"

The group exchanged glances. One flicked his cigarette butt towards them while the other smashed his bottle to the wall. Figures behind curtains disappeared, candles were being put out one by one. The man in the middle who spoke to them crossed his arms then rubbed his hands together. "Well then, dandy. Let's do it your way."

They met in the middle, the narrowest part of the street, shoulders hunched, knees bent slightly. Valerie peered at them through a crevice in a wall. She knew something had to happen soon. The click-clack of boots, the terrible loud breathings, each beat of hearts terribly pulsing. All the windows were dark now. They were left alone.

Then nothing happened. A voice let loose a grumble, as if fatigued, then it became a snarl and the men ran into the street crying where they came from. The lingering smoke and the bitterness of beer clung to Valerie's lips. She could not dismiss the feeling of dissonance, ever so slight, yet perceivable; the chilling and disquieting dread which left Valerie inexplicably drained.

"What happened?" Valerie asked out of breath, hurrying to Mircalla's side. She broke into a voice of shrill desperation.

"My sweet, curious Valerie," she purred, the moonlight turning her eyes to gold. "I don't particularly feel good about my actions but I wasn't going to let a group of sots taunt us." She offered her hand. A silent invitation, the sight of which ran right through her.

20

THEY TRUDGED BACK UP the hill but not to Vertigo Peaks. Valerie walked around like someone in a trance, crisscrossing the streets and imagining what she had wanted to do. She did not grasp what was forward, nor did she care. Mircalla was leading the way again and Valerie was struck by the wonder of her, a force of life she had never seen before, held at her bay, filled with greediness to the brim, which turned then to craving.

They reached a vast clearing and Valerie's eyes swept the edge of it. She knew the woods. She knew beyond that stretched her home and the peaks. Yet, she still glided to the shadows to listen to its humming voice. The place seemed bare at first, only a blanket of snow as company, no place to hide. Upon a closer look, Valerie noticed, her throat rattling, figures slowly dancing at the end of a path. Fire had put a tranquil glow on their outlines. She half expected to recognize them before approaching; arms linked, bodies in gentle repose. But these were wanderers, who ceased to wish upon perseverance, revived only by the mere passing of a scenery.

"You shall be nearer to me than you have ever been."

Mircalla took hold of her arm. She recognized the soft lull of her voice, but everything else was drowning in darkness. She felt her cold breath on her neck, inhaling before withdrawing her arm, and an ache in her teeth made her wince in pain. When she finally saw the dancing figures from the flare, her wounds itched again.

"Who are they?" Valerie tried to whisper, but the sensation was so strong that her throat tightened. Her memory faltered. Had she seen these people before? She searched the faces to focus on, but everything within her called for one distinct memory.

She had felt the soft crust of trees on her back before, pine needles pricking her bare feet, a distinct pluck of ardor, and her throat ripped apart. She remembered the screams, the terrifying thump of struggle, a particular sort of chase, air rippling through the nape of her neck. Black spots hovered before her eyes.

Mircalla caught her before she fell.

"What is this place? Why did you bring me here?"

"Valerie," Mircalla's voice sliced through the stillness, "There's something I must tell you... or *show* you."

Slack expressions and mouthfuls of blood. There was a combination of metallic crispness and burnt meat in the air. The fire subdued and Valerie saw the faces smeared with blood, pieces of skin dangling from teeth. A girl was convulsing, a pool of blood spewing from her gash and over her limbs, spread and twisted in weird positions, all mangled and torn open like a bag.

Mircalla tugged on her arm. "I am not of this world, my dear. Not of flesh or blood. I rise beyond the grave." Valerie could feel her cheeks were hot. Her eyes were blazing with a sensation, darker still, that crept stealthily up her legs. The swell of her tongue full of thick desire.

"A vampire, they named me. But you know me as the beast. The plague bearer. They found me and illuminated my path. I don't have to be alone anymore."

Mircalla knelt before the girl, who was not convulsing anymore but regarded them with glassy eyes nevertheless, and dipped her chin to her chest cavity, ribs exposed. It was a moment of waking remembrance, producing the familiar sensation of disgust and excitement. The small movements of her head, her devouring mouth reflected in those dark, glassy eyes.

Mircalla's head tilted back sharply. She extended an arm, a slick and crimson brilliance in her smile. Her nose was encrusted with blood, as if it sprung from her, part of her. Every nerve in Valerie's body was buzzing and bright; a familiar energy grew in her fingertips. Mircalla lured her, fascinated her to the edges of her sanity, a sign that turned Valerie into a slow and deliberate creature. Here, there was nothing sweeter.

"Come closer, Valerie," Mircalla said. "This you shall become, this you shall crave more."

"Taste it, Valerie," the group tempted. She had never wanted to dive straight to the bottom of entrails before and the need to soothe her frayed nerves with blood had never been this imminent. She knelt next to Mircalla, the flash behind her eyes blinding and unwavering.

She sank, with torrents of blood like tar, as if exploding in the darkness of the woods. She used to be a blur but images flashed against her closed eyes—Mircalla's red face, the crackle of bones, the boy's lantern.

"It was you," Valerie gasped. Blood still gushed out of the girl but she was already full. Mircalla cupped her face and she could almost smell her unnatural breath. She could not help but lean closer, lingering on the edge of her comforting familiarity.

"I was a monster then. I had no control. When my teeth sank into your neck... I could have killed you. I did not know how to control this... urge."

"Was this why you were sick?"

"Yes," Mircalla whispered. "That's why I was looking for you. I was delirious. All I could hear was your name. I was never a lost traveler, you see, I was just trying to find you. It was hard controlling myself around you however, and I'm afraid I failed time and time again."

"What do you mean?"

Mircalla's face took on that pinched look. A sidelong glance was enough to shrink Valerie. "Tell me," Valerie insisted. They left the corpse there and walked back to the path.

"I was afraid. I thought I was never going to see you again."

A young man tugged at Valerie's arm before she could speak, twisting the skin until her eyes watered.

"Taste it," he demanded. "You shall be one with us."

Valerie plunged her head again, this time with hesitance, and drank the blood. It was foul, cloying, and lukewarm, like a cup of tea forgotten on a windowsill, and Valerie found herself crying. And though Mircalla's eyes were on her; Valerie's hand, like a peregrine's black talon, gripped the girl's heart, and caused her to feel, at the thought of death, terror. The young man patted her back, as if celebrating her, and Valerie rolled to her side heaving, ashes sticking to her lashes.

"Come, darling, sit up."

Mircalla poured ice cold water over her head and wiped the blood off her face. She cried over the shock and cringed as the blood dripped onto her lap. Above her, the sky was darker than she was used to seeing, which she connected to those early days of waiting when she hoped to catch a glimpse of Mircalla, and the sight of it filled Valerie with trepidation.

"Did you...turn me into a vampire?" Valerie asked, tongue wedged in the corner of her mouth. She failed to keep anxiety from her voice. "Is this what I'm feeling? A morbid hunger that I'll starve for the rest of my life?"

Mircalla was so silent, she wondered whether she heard her. The air was unnaturally heavy, and the woods remained a gulf of space; absolute and silver-patched. Her sleek stillness washed over her.

"Pain and pleasure usually have the same sound." Mircalla's voice was hoarse and muffled. "The horror of seeing the heart of your lover on a silver plate is also thrilling. Deep in your bones, you already know. Matter to matter. Blood gives blood. You'd rather die than not eat away what you love."

Armed with a newfound consciousness, and not for the first time, Valerie was left in awe of this insatiable thirst, the kind that did not adjust or bend, only giving temporary releases by turns. Nothing seemed to stop this appetite; no amount of shock or terror could constraint this outreaching burst of bloodlust. It coursed through her veins, despite Valerie not being aware of its properties, and Mircalla's voice was full of longing, full of rueful desiring, full of suffering and beauty.

She needed not saving, but giving in. The townspeople would never love her. Her husband would remain a relentless servant of his hollow crown. In the meantime, she would part the veil and look at the other side, just for anything to happen.

21

MIRCALLA HAD WRAPPED HER arms around her neck, smiling, laughing; her mouth wandering around her face with that acrid smell like a lighthouse searching for a boat as they moved forward step by step. Valerie took it all in.

"Let's get you cleaned." Mircalla gestured at her dress. Valerie looked at herself. The world was spinning faster than her eye could catch. Was she drunk? She recalled the hue of the girl's chest cavity and her convulsions. It was like she had never opened her eyes before. The image set her on fire as yet another silence engulfed them in midnight blue. Mircalla slid her hand back in hers, cold and restless as ever, and led her to Vertigo Peaks.

Once they were in the house, stumbling upstairs like a child scared of a parent's scolding, lips pursed and fearful of every creaking noise, they glided past Valerie's door and made an abrupt turn.

"Come," Mircalla said, "it's just you and me."

Something slithered inside Valerie's chest, as if a snake coiled itself around her, two white fangs piercing through heart, not in misery but in delight, and she followed Mircalla into the dark hall.

Dust fell off the room—candle wax, moth-eaten books, hearth. It filtered the light as the candles glowed dully, as though afraid of their presence, spreading a heavy moldy smell in the cold air. It became easier to see Mircalla's expression as her eyes adjusted to the candlelight, looking fluid, as if she could not decide what shape to possess.

The dwindling fire set sparks on her pale cheeks, her eyes lustrous and intent, her lust rekindled. Valerie was aware of everything, the frantic beat of her heart, the heat pulsing on her skin, yet she dared not touch her. All she could do was stand there with her trembling hands, return Mircalla's stare, drunk with the anticipation of a moment long waited for.

Mircalla took a step forward. "Let me help you," she said. "Your coat must be heavy." Her body was all Valerie could see, she filled the periphery of her vision with such ardor and care that her chest ached, for she had known that these sensations lived in her too, once betrayed and cursed. She was tired of fighting them. Not anymore.

She took deep gulps of crisp air. The smoke made it to her lungs. Mircalla approached faster, her head hung low, as if prowling, but Valerie stood still as she turned her around and unbuttoned her coat. There was only a rustling of fabric, a flash of moonlight, and Mircalla's shallow bursts of breath upon her. Mircalla's hands were slow—intentionally slow—and when her coat dropped on the floor, she shivered.

Blood had already dried on Mircalla's lips and she reached for the rusty taste. The hat and hair pins gone, her hair cascaded down her back and Mircalla wrapped a lock around her finger as she kissed her. For a fleeting moment, everything but her disappeared. There was nothing else to lean on but Mircalla's glowing body.

"If I am to be one of your kind." Valerie exhaled. "Will you stand by me? Because frankly, I am at my wits' end. I can barely move."

Mircalla tipped her chin with a triumphant smile then she pressed her lips where the itch burned. She licked the salt in her wound and Valerie could barely stand, resting on her chest with her hands laced around her face, closer and closer in a swirl of emotions. Her heart was thundering in her chest, but she was only aware of where Mircalla's lips pressed against.

They were crimsoned and shaking.

"I'm afraid," Mircalla whispered, a tender smile dancing on her lips. "I don't have the strength in me to let you go. I can't control it. I would rip my heart off its birdcage and hand it over to you if it meant we could stay like this forever. How can I ever let you go, my dear Valerie, the heart of my soul, when you have given me the world?"

The quaver in Mircalla's voice made her shiver. She was cut out from the draughts of her body, inhaling mist and blood. Mircalla unbuttoned her trousers, never taking her eyes off her, then looked at her blood soaked shirt. Her fingers were clumsy, unable to move quicker, and she faltered with every motion.

Mircalla swore under her breath as she fumbled another button. "I don't mind admitting that I'm nervous, but my gosh, I am terrible at this."

"Let me help," Valerie whispered, as much for herself as for her. She kissed Mircalla again, still looking into her eyes, unbuttoned her shirt to where the swell of her belly began and kissed her again. She was caught between Mircalla and the bed and realized that the shirt was stiff with blood, slight sweat patches under her arms, and she dropped it on the pile with the rest of her clothes. Mircalla pulled off her stockings, and Valerie could not help but sob. Deeper her hands pulled and pulled and heat mounted on her stomach, her breasts, setting her ribs aflame. Mircalla was cold and it was as if she reached a mountaintop, frozen and brumal as her skin recognized hers.

She stood before her with nothing but her corset and sighed heavily as she clutched her neck. Mircalla's gaze rendered her all but invisible and Valerie was about to explode. Mircalla motioned her to approach, lips parted and lids heavy with unbounded lust. Valerie, her own face flushed and too aware of its building energy, was seized by surging adoration.

"My corset...Please—" Valerie began, growing rough and impatient. She gave a low moan of despair and shut her eyes close. It was impossible to handle the weight of this crush, collapsing into herself like a great dome of passion and she did not care if it was a sin, corrupting her soul and shaping her body into a carnal museum. It was exhilarating to find herself this animated next to the woman who she pronounced only a guest a few weeks ago.

Mircalla traced a finger down her corset, the swell of her chest pressing lightly against her back, and planted kisses beside her ear, and said, "You're lucky I'm good with laces." Valerie could hear her smile as her lips followed a meandering path, kissing her with greater hunger and confidence. She untied the bow first, then loosened the lace, the weight pulled off her waist. She stroked her cheek with her chin and leaned over her shoulder. Her fingers moved faster this time, the sound of unhooking echoing in the room.

"You are so warm," she said, and with each word, her lips brushed against hers. "And I envy the heart that beats inside you, the skin that wraps you. I loathe the breadth of air that touches you, the morning frost that sees you before I do. But these will not keep me from trying."

"Then, let me see you try."

Mircalla carried her to the bed; she was still fully dressed. Valerie sucked in a sharp breath as the cold sheets greeted her and her eyes were still drawn on Mircalla. Her hair was cascading down in a silky wave, and she looked up at her with a knowing smirk. Valerie felt a jolt of electricity run through her as their eyes met. Her heart was racing with anticipation as Mircalla pulled her closer for another kiss and their bodies were pressed together, exploring each other under shadows; Mircalla's moans soft in her mouth, like the touch of a butterfly, and under the pressure of her tongue, everything was simple.

And if she was on the brink of collapse, it did not matter. It was like drifting off to sleep, being embraced by this creature, dashed by blood and inspiration, and the gushing chill of her body overwhelmed her. Valerie's hand settled on the small of her back, tight and steady, as Mircalla climbed on top of her. She quickly stripped off her vest and shirt, threw them across the room, and her hand was moving up and down Valerie's chest. She was aching from wanting more, the dizzying sweetness of the moment had fueled her hunger. Mircalla had the same disoriented look. It was as if they were both passing from one turbulent state to another, wandering around the earth without the knowledge of the other, and as they now melted in each other's hands, against their lips, the days spent in separation seemed like a privation. A collision of order. Wanting someone this profoundly, giving into the delicious yearning, both monstrous and exalting, or admitting sanguine defeats drenched in her lover's sweat would never be a compromise if she had never been married. It would be a eulogy.

For her, there had always been a violent gap between her history of suffering and her dreams for the future, for she could not overcome the gap without being destroyed by it. She had clung to the promise in her name and was ruined by it. She would bury the past all night long and still not be done because she didn't feel she had a right to forget her losses, or insist upon marking herself in the present. She was a monument made to despair and regret. Still, despite her reservations, she could not stop dreaming about growing new roots, right on this bed as Mircalla's lips wandered on her collarbone and down to her breasts. The saddest cadence of her voice became a guttural plea, alive by the touch of another woman, and the tender belief that all would be well.

"Please." Valerie writhed in pleasure. Without a word, Mircalla buried her hand to Valerie's neck, wrapping her arms around her, and she felt a sharp pain that seared her mouth. Mircalla had sunk her teeth deep into her flesh, leaving her with a growing need to be closer and closer.

The blood was draining from her body, but the rush was more palpable, consuming, and addictive. Her body caught up with the sentiment quickly, hurling itself in her direction, her back tight like an arrow, and Valerie knew, with such precision that almost made her blind, that she was under Mircalla Karnstein's spell, body and soul. She was given over to the night, became a raging beast of prey herself, born from nowhere but her sighs. What she knew about herself had been crafted from the account of others, the smacking lips and pointed ears. No, no. She was, indeed, a beautiful and reckless experiment of being, loving, and wanting.

Valerie was ravenous and uncontained, much like her lover who convulsed above her, latching on to the quietest parts of her body, spreading her limbs open as much as she could and Valerie couldn't bring herself to resist. Mircalla pulled back for a moment, her lips stained with Valerie's blood, a site of her new origin. She feared the moment would be lost and Mircalla would leave, but she leaned in closer and gave her a taste of her own blood.

A stream of color shimmering on her skin, carnations blooming on her chest. Valerie sobbed. She felt brave and noble, bewildered and confused by this undefined lust in her heart. It bred new questions, but nothing remained when she was under Mircalla's gaze as she kissed along her stomach until she reached the waistband of her drawers.

With a wicked grin, she pulled it down, exposing the heat, and Mircalla nuzzled against her skin, following the curve of her inner thighs, then moved up, ready to taste her to the core. She kissed and settled on the top of her, stroking her thighs longer and longer, and teasing with her breath, before finally diving in with her tongue. It was lovely to look down; a tickling, seducing sensation, and her lover's hair tangled in her fingers, eyes gone bright, fingers curling up just the right way to dangle her off the precipice.

"Mircalla..."

She was beside herself, her breath rising and falling rapidly, turning into dreadful sighs. She was slick with sweat and blood, wanting to reach out and press Mircalla's head harder but Mircalla crawled up her body and kissed the punctures.

"Did you like it?" Her breath was hot against Valerie's ear. She moaned as though she was washed by heavenly light. A place unstated and undefined—the threshold of untamed encounters, splitting at the heart of meaning, searching for vitality; at the same time, unsettling the notion of getting it right, stripping it down so only the pangs of desire remain.

Valerie nodded, suffused with heat and the tangy taste sliding down her tongue, heaving and at a loss for words. Her voice was nothing more than a weak wheezing sound. Mircalla laughed and curled her fingers deeper.

"I pray you won't keep quiet tonight, my love."

Valerie gripped the sheets with one hand and covered her mouth with the other to stop the screaming as their bodies landed with a quick release, collapsing onto the bed, names lingering on their lips. Valerie was devoid of any sense, unconscious and limp with pleasure that lifted her like crushing waves, and the moonlight shone on her face with such intensity that she thought she was dead.

22

THE NIGHT PASSED IN peace. Mircalla folded her hands on the shallow pit in her back, trailing a finger along Valerie's flushed face, and they laid quietly. But there was an unpassing sensation that slithered under Valerie's skin. It crept in silently at first, as sleep creeps in after supper, like something rumbling beneath the bed, then it stabbed as it went, tearing her apart limb by limb. Mircalla noticed her unrest. Her face was grave, contorted with agony, and Valerie twisted back and forth like a wild animal.

"It hurts," she said. Mircalla kissed and embraced her again and again, as tears ran slowly down her cheeks. This particular sensation, Valerie feared, was finding its violent entrance and sickening something inside. By morning, she was deeply bewildered, and nestled up even closer to Mircalla. She squeezed her eyes shut. Her teeth were chattering; her feet felt like icicles under the quilt.

When her body finally stopped, Mircalla leaned over her shoulder and gave her a kiss.

"Mircalla, will you forgive me if I ask you a question?"

Her imploring eyes gave Mircalla a pause. It was still cold in the room, the frost on the windows, and Valerie was grateful that Mircalla had kindled the fire to keep her warm. But she, leaning dejectedly on her lover's arm as she smoothed her hair, was perplexed by this incurable coldness that overshadowed everything. A great vapor of her tea swirled beside the bed like a string and she had tried to warm her swollen fingertips with the cup. But it was all in vain.

"Was this the sensation that possessed you—prickling, bruising aching in the heart? Were you this far from well when you came to us? Do you think me very ill?"

She looked at her, Mircalla's smile faded.

"I was lost. I have nothing left of those days but a terrible dream and it demands, most certainly, a desire for silence. But my love, my dear Valerie, I came here with the same feelings that disturb you now. I-I think you not ill, the recovery will be quick, quick. Your heart will ease. I am sure."

It was, perhaps, far easier to bring the memory of Mircalla's illness to mind and plunge herself into abject misery than seeking remedy for herself. Yet, Valerie couldn't find it in her heart to turn away from Mircalla and invite others to crowd the room with their narrowed eyes and uncertain words. She did not want recovery unless it came from Mircalla, who knew her heart and soul and all its anxieties. A minute later, her throat closed with a stifling sensation—as if her heart were larger than her chest, frozen and queasy. It produced in her a feeling of unquenchable thirst: a ragged mouth and distressed, shaking hands; a similar languor which once possessed her dear guest.

Mircalla, on the contrary, was glowing. Her face was radiant and charming in the muted winter light, bursts of sparks covered last night's lust but Valerie felt she could ignite it if she held her close. Her wild hair was disheveled in places and her lips looked so plump that it turned almost a deep maroon color.

"I wonder if this will keep you warm." Mircalla shifted and pulled Valerie on top of her. She pouted, as if in deep thought, then a wide smile flitted across her face. "My findings tell me it will, based on how rosy-cheeked you were yesterday."

"Mircalla—" She gasped, words stuck in her throat. She dug her nails into Mircalla's round shoulders, trying to balance herself, then leaned on her elbows. Their lashes almost touched, and she studied the violent circles under her eyes, traced the faint tremble of her lips, and heard air leaving her mouth. Mircalla lifted her hips a little bit and they looked at each other for a moment. Must she remember her mistakes, or hold deep inside her a piece of lacking? She wanted to let Mircalla catch her in her arms, settle between her legs, and keep her awake. She wanted happiness, eventually, and to never miss a moment again. She dipped her chin to kiss Mircalla on the side of her mouth and Mircalla tilted her head and kissed her softly, cold and salty, like the sea. She never belonged to herself before this moment.

Valerie was licking the gap on her former guest's chest when Ethan's voice echoed through the hallway. They exchanged glances with the precision of a couple, and the realization of which made her almost smile, yet her husband's voice kept her away from the fondness of her thoughts.

"Valerie, where the hell are you? Valerie!"

Mircalla pushed her off the bed and she stumbled toward where Mircalla's nightgown laid on top of the heap their clothes made last night. Thankfully, the dress seemed at least decent enough to put on. It was not spotless, yet crusted blood stains were easy to hide if she let her hair down her shoulders.

She peeked out the keyhole but the hall was completely dark. It occurred to her that he might be waiting by the door, ready to spit on her face and shake his fist. Her hand froze on the knob, and there was a loud click as she turned it. She held her breath, keeping it turned, waiting to see if there was any sound—a sharp breath, feet stomping, a squeak of vengeance. Nothing.

"Ethan? Where are you?" she called in the dark and walked for a while, feeling the damp walls and peeling wallpaper to find her way.

"Where were you? I checked your chambers two times already and have been screaming your name at the top of my lungs like a damned fisherman."

Valerie could not see anything, but heard the sound of rasping, labored breathing and smelled the taint of smoke on the walls.

"I haven't been up for long, Ethan. I was just chatting with Miss Karnstein, wishing the lady a good day."

If she could see, she would swear that a cloud of disbelief passed his face, yet he said nothing, only stood before her as if unsure of what to do, the whites of his eye gleaming like rotten eggs, then pulled her into the dappled light on the landing. He was shaking his head, and then pinched the bridge of his nose before speaking.

"Yes, fine. Well done. Brilliant work as a hostess, much better than the last time people were in our house, if I may. But...that's not the point." He shook his head again, his bushy mustache also rippling. Valerie noticed how he bent his neck like a hook, as he usually did in the pursuit of a zealous occasion. It was difficult to keep her face straight. "Cecilia and her little group want to stop by for tea this afternoon."

Valerie scoffed. "What for? To taunt me or to flaunt their unmatched brilliance?"

"Do not be childish, it's very unbecoming of you." He shifted his weight from one leg to another, apparently thinking about the same possibility himself. "Besides, their butler was not as morose as usual, Ethel said. He even tugged the corners of his mouth into a smile, apparently, which petrified her, poor thing."

Seeing Valerie unmoved by the news, Ethan cleared his throat and assumed an air of overexcitement to justify the proposal. His eyes almost bulged out of his sockets and his shoulders trembled under the weight of his bouncing head. "It's an olive branch, a peace treaty, or whatever you call it, you see? I'm most confident we'll see some progress."

"On what exactly?" Valerie folded her arms.

"Cecilia has not been very supportive of our marriage and my power, but this is a step forward. She knows she made a mistake and that no matter what happens, what calamity befalls us, people cherish what I've done for them. They know I devoted my life for their prosperity and I think Cecilia understands this now."

He grabbed her hand with a slip of fever, like he had never touched her before—loutishly, without affection or need. He always had a tendency to take and claim, with a precise aversion to what he could not possess, and Valerie always stood beside him crestfallen and waxy. She drew her hand back.

"If you believe so," she said in a weak voice. His presence was draining the life force out of her. "I'll let Miss Karnstein know."

The ticking heart of Vertigo Peaks was calm as a sparrow. Valerie did not know what to make of this stillness; it was strange, like a cut on the lip, standing in the middle of a room without the quakes of the manor-house under her feet, the gruff noises and exhalations, as though something crucial had disappeared and its absence left the scene disappointing.

She had been informed by Ethel, who carried a tiny scribbled note with burnt edges, that she was to meet with Cecilia and her cohort alone. "This is a special occasion. Visiting female friends would be bored out of their minds if I were there. Make the most of it."

Valerie smoothed a crease on her champagne gold tea gown, adjusting the ruffles on the lace of her bodice and sleeve cuffs, pushing back the coiling longer train trimmed in black velvet. Getting rid of the dried blood under her nails proved to be a disaster. Likewise, she had to wash her mouth over and over again to erase any trace of crusty skin and tissues. The morbid fascination of the night had disappeared and left a grotesque form in its wake, riddled with the remains of her hunger. Nevertheless, she still looked lavishly feminine in her dress, and like her husband wanted, with a disposition ever amiable.

"Have they arrived?"

Mircalla wrapped an arm around her waist and kissed her cheek. Valerie hurriedly stepped aside, blushed and throat clenched, and shrieked, "Miss Karnstein!"

"What?" Mircalla answered in the same tone, sneaking in another kiss. "He already left."

"Someone will see us, don't! Ethel is probably around."

Mircalla, laughing heartily, pressed her in a gentle embrace and leaned her cheek against hers then sighed. "I miss you."

"I'm right here."

"I miss you still."

Valerie shifted position and cupped Mircalla's face in her hands. Her eyes were bright and clear, and she had a silver glow around the edges of her body as if lit by a lantern from within. The light washed over her, tickling her finger tips, and before words formed in her mouth, she tipped Mircalla's chin and brushed her lips against hers. She wanted it to be polite and quick, a shadow of something greater that they shared last night, but Mircalla did not let go.

Valerie had never dreamed of this, of stealing moments away from the watchful house, frolicking in decaying rooms, and smiling from ear to ear. She had never looked at someone like this before, she dreaded meeting the intensity of her gaze in mirrors, for it was intense and sometimes left her sore. But, as long as Mircalla was here, she was a friend, a lover. She was home.

It was her own name echoing back in the shape of Mircalla's body; it was a return, reclaim, self-knowledge to love her. She would be like her one day: a vampire. With its vitality and blood-lust and mystique and a firm belief in herself that won't be taken away.

When she broke the kiss, it was to say, "I love you." But moments like these were always fragile and disappointment settled in her chest like a heavy stone. A creak down the hall, barely audible, shattered the spell. Valerie pulled away, eyes sharp, and laced her fingers together.

"A carriage is approaching the drive, madam."

As soon as Ethel fell silent, Valerie heard the crunch of gravel and snow, accompanied by a roar of laughter. When Ethel opened the door, Valerie saw four carriages with horses like mountains that were controlled by young men with smudges of mushroom-colored strands of hair on their upper lips instead of mustaches, wiping the sweat with the back of their tight gloves, puffs of breath visible in the air. It was hard for her to not be taciturn or morose as the horsemen helped the ladies step out in their embellished gowns and powdered faces.

Valerie's attention was attested by the sight of Cecilia Harker. She advanced to the doorway as the host and noticed the healthy flush on her guest's cheeks. A rich velvet cloak covered her back as flakes descended around her, as though she was a subject of a painting. She was laughing still as they approached Valerie, a glowing smirk stretching the skin like a dough, and cupped by fine jewelry. The lighthearted conversation carried on as the sound of carriage wheels and the galloping hooves died away in the winter air.

"Valerie, dear! It has been a long time since I had the pleasure of your company!" Cecilia raised her arms and hugged her. "Frankly, I am upset with you for not visiting us again." She pulled away from the hug to look at her. Valerie was numb with shock, unable to return her guest's interest, and by the time she managed to command her tongue to speak, they were already in the drawing room, surrounded by the scent of freshly baked goods that filled the room, accompanied by the warm crackling of a cozy fireplace.

Mixed in with these warm smells was the waft of sugary, thick perfume that caught its way up to Valerie.

Cecilia Harker was acting unlike herself—without boiling anger or snide remarks about the state of her house or her looks. Valerie struggled not to raise a brow and instead chose to purse her lips for a while before her silence could be seen as rude.

"It is so pleasant to have you here at Vertigo Peaks," she finally muttered, "I hope you had a pleasant ride."

"Indeed. Thank you for being so generous and inviting us all." Cecilia gestured at her friends. Lady Amelia, Lady Catherine, and Lady Evelyn waved at her at the same time. The more she looked at them, the more they looked like bad copies of Cecilia Harker. Their stiff movements only showed vigor when she was speaking and they stared at the wall whenever conversation shifted away from her.

"Such an exquisite place! You've done a marvelous job bringing this old treasure back to its glory, I must say. Everyone had been worried about its...derelict state, you know. Ah." She sighed, "It feels like yesterday when I was sitting in this very room with your husband and his sister." Then her gloved hands flew to her mouth as if she had said something obscene. "My apologies...What a babbler I am! But you must understand, Valerie, it is because I missed the ease of our conversations. I do not mean to open old wounds."

"We all are saddened by the passing of his sister and whom, I am told, I look very much alike," Valerie said to cut the subject short. The only ease Valerie had ever gotten from Cecilia Harker's conversation was when Valerie left the dinner party. What was she trying to do? Valerie narrowed her eyes. It was too late to look away.

"Passing?" Cecilia almost spat out her tea. "No, my dear. She went *missing*. The poor soul was never found, nor a body recovered, so everyone naturally assumed she was dead after months of search. But... Yes, she went missing. Not a usual demise one might say."

Valerie perked up. The ladies were whispering among themselves like a council, nibbling on a piece of cookie or gulping tea, electrified by the apparent misinformation Valerie had received.

"No need to fret, Mrs. Harker," she added in a low voice, "How did it happen? She could not have disappeared into thin air, right? Something must have precipitated these horrendous events."

Her guest nodded in an understanding way and leaned over the table. She had a sandwich in one hand, a teacup in the other.

"Is it really hard to tell, Mrs. Vertigo?" She tipped her head back, looking at the walls lined with portraits, hunting prizes, and the scrolls of peeled wallpaper lying on the floor. Even in the afternoon, it was dark. Yet, Valerie could see the layers of old and yellowed wallpaper with strips of stamped flowers, the faded corners. A shiver ran through her spine as Cecilia poured herself another cup of tea with a dash of lemon and a spoonful of sugar.

"I wish to take no part in private affairs. They are often trifling and not nuanced enough to keep me engaged. But, your family, madam, is different, isn't that so?" Her knowing smirk was annoying as ever but more importantly, her certainty made Valerie's skin crawl. "The circumstances that led to the disappearance of the young lady have never been a mystery to us—to those who knew them both well. Your husband and his little sister."

"What do you mean?" Mircalla raised her cup and took a sip. She did not realize she had been this thirsty.

"There were rumors, or rather stories, about their strenuous relationship. But do not be mistaken! They were a wonderful pair in the public, in the company of others. They were both devoted to this town as their sole duty, working day and night to make this hellish piece of land habitable, running auctions and organizing charities for those in need. It was when they were alone, or distant from the crowds, the most discordant arguments were inflicted."

She chuckled. She had a wild gleam in her eyes that scared Valerie. "Now I can see, in many ways, it was like having two appointed conductors for the same symphony; oblivious to each other's sheets or movements in the air. One can never suppose it will end well. Such a waste! Mr. Emery Vertigo himself seemed to be indifferent to this supposed affliction. We very much never saw him set foot outside the house, but you know how talks spread like wildfire."

"But why?" Valerie kept asking to herself, then realized she was saying it out loud too. It was difficult enough to wrap her mind around the meticulously crafted secrecy of her husband and his family. It was even more difficult to comprehend the possibility of jealousy and rivalry between siblings.

A few minutes later, Cecilia Harker broke a shortbread biscuit in half, once again high-spirited and flamboyant, and resumed talking. "Let us talk of things light and merry, please! I am growing tired." She patted the back of her hand. "I am planning the annual ball of the season and there's nothing in this world that would make me happier if you were my guest of honor."

Valerie reeled back in her seat, barely able to open her mouth to breathe like a fish out of the water, her eyes looking for marks of usual ridicule and scorn, yet Mrs. Harker was busy eating the second half of her biscuit, holding butter in her free hand.

Valerie glanced at Mircalla. She was sitting listlessly on the other side of the large table, shaking her head in unison every now and then. She did not touch a single cake or cucumber sandwich. A similar confusion pervaded her gaze and the corners of her mouth drifted downward.

"I know we had a rough start," Mrs. Harker continued like she didn't pause, an edge of regret in her voice, "There's no way to put it better: I have been a scoundrel. I have been an awful mentor, let alone a confidant, and threw you to the wolves. I mistreated you in my house and broke your heart. For all that, I am deeply sorry. I want to atone for my sins, if you let me, and put us on the right track."

Valerie began to stutter, glancing nervously at the room. She could not make sense of Mrs. Harker's drastic change of manner, the most placid and kind she had ever seen from her, and could not help but wonder if there was a deeper reason underlying it.

"I am most thankful," she replied at last, pressing her wedding ring to her flesh, finding a sudden yet ambitious impulse to peek behind Cecilia's skin and bones. "I'd be honored."

Cecilia clapped her hands in response, jumping in her seat, a smudge of butter on top of her lips. "That's wonderful! Did you hear that ladies? My goodness, we have a lot to do! You must join us for shopping. My tailor has the latest fashion materials. From ribbons to petticoats and feathers!"

Then the room took notice of her cheers and carried on with the laughter. The room seemed much brighter as the reflecting light of snow poured through the paned windows, slanting at the edge of their table, flooding their figures in a cool glow. It was only Mircalla who was left in the dark, appearing between floating dust motes when Valerie had a chance to look, arms folded, inscrutable in her brooding silence.

23

VALERIE WAS ON THE top of her dresser, giggling and breathing in Mircalla's mouth. Moonbeams shone through the naked branches of trees, casting broken shapes through the dusty panes. She stirred. Mircalla was all angles and shadows, a figment of her imagination perhaps, and she could not help but feel what she reached out for was long gone. Still, her lips parted in a sigh as she held onto Mircalla's waist to catch her breath who then flashed her teeth and pulled her in for a kiss.

"Look at me," Mircalla said, kneeling before her. The floor creaked under her steps. The vibrating thud of her knees scraping the floor rang in Valerie's ears. For so long, Valerie had dreamt of leaving this life behind, perturbed and aware of what rested in her was apathy, yet longing to swarm around bodies she did not know like a homesick ghost, eager to skin her elbows and knees, so that she may touch someone for the first time.

As she inhaled, the woman before her shifted position, and it was impossible not to dissolve away in this fondness. At the same time, Ethan said, "Keep your eyes on me." But his lips weren't moving. "I dare you."

So Valerie nibbled on her husband's severed finger. She did not question when or where it appeared. It must have been in her hand all her life, in a blaze, sealed behind the coldness of January. She was meant to be here, cradled by her bloodthirsty lover, and sucking on her husband's flesh until the hard bone grated against her teeth. Even then, she pushed the finger down her throat, feeling the cold touch of his wedding ring on her tongue, her gaze fixed on his ashen face.

He was just a few steps away from her, rocking back and forth on his heels, as if drunk. He put pressure on where his finger stretched a moment ago. Beads of sweat shimmered on his forehead but his eyes did not falter: spawning hatred, vicious, vindictive.

Meanwhile, Mircalla's hands were making their way up Valerie's woolen stockings, head buried under her billowing skirt, and Valerie felt a sharp pang in her stomach, resisting the urge to grab Mircalla by the hair and press her wandering lips harder to her trembling skin.

Ethan's voice thundered. "You're a crook," he said. "A heathen, whore." He attempted to lurch forward, raised his arms to tumble her down, but blood streaked down his shirt, and his body failed him. He leaned against the wall, breathing hard.

Valerie continued to gorge on his finger, though slightly nauseous. The flesh warmed on her lips, blood dripping down her chest and into her dress, and she swallowed another chewy, sour bite.

Mircalla's hasty fingers tickled her calves as she tugged on her drawers. She lifted her hips while the fabric loosened around her ankles and her lover's lips followed the path her hands wandered and Valerie moaned every time she left burning kisses. She looked down, the bulge of Mircalla's head fluttered her skirt like ripples on a lake. Her cheek pressed against the inside of her thigh, roaming over the soft spot where Valerie had been aching the most. A jolt of electricity ran through her as Mircalla tore her skirt apart and their eyes met.

It should not feel like paradise, Valerie thought, the last piece of the gnarly finger dangling from the tip of her lips. But when Mircalla was this close, her breath like crashing waves against her skin, slick with sweat and warm with kisses, Valerie only wanted to move her hands and invite her deeper inside, where every fiber of her existence exploded with one name.

Mircalla Karnstein.

Restless and brimming with ecstasy, Valerie grabbed the corners of the nightstand. She swallowed the last piece of the finger, the hairs on it sticking to her teeth, the veins soft and chewy, the marrow salacious and sweet. His ring fell and thudded against the floor, sending a web of scarlet in every direction and Ethan faded from her view.

Mircalla always touched her as she was. She was never incomplete, never unfilled. Free from the torment of her own angles, Valerie truly felt alive and boundless. She did not have a reason to complicate things: She wanted Mircalla, she needed Mircalla. She wanted to collapse, lay her foundation in front of her so she may pace her untended soil. She was overgrown with wishful lust and only Mircalla could absolve her clean.

Her lover looked up with a wicked grin. Valerie could only gasp at the sight of her. Her hair cascaded down her back in twined curls, the gleam in her eye reflected the same need. Her legs hung from Mircalla's shoulders like vines winding around each other's stems, and Valerie's heart raced against her chest as Mircalla buried her face between her legs. She was teasing her as she always did. Her breath was quick and loud on her stomach before she finally dived in with her tongue. In that moment, she quit lingering. She was here, and she had always been. Burying her hands in Mircalla's hair, she arched her back, moaning loudly as Mircalla licked her and she felt like she was about to drown, inescapably writhing around Mircalla's lips.

Mircalla's tongue flicked over her clitoris. It was as if she had lived on the edge of the world until now and the jump only made the cliff look pitiable. She was falling apart, screaming and shaking with pleasure. The heat inside her built until she could not take anymore, a thousand needles devoutly crawling her skin.

24

HER MEETINGS WITH MRS. Harker had gone beyond ordinary shopping trips. Cecilia sometimes invited her to her home and they chatted about the state of the town, treading warily around the subjects that concerned Vertigo Peaks and her reputation. In the company of warm tea and buttery scones, Valerie spent hours and was most often kept by her host to stay for supper.

They also made a habit of visiting other ladies of the group together, sharing a carriage, girdled by the windswept plains as they, inch by inch, climbed up the snow-clad hills, and the crunch of ice upon steel filled the air. Their conversation slowly found a rhythm—expanding without hindrance, occasionally defensive, yet still remarkably comforting. Valerie was usually the listening party. Emboldened by the urgency of the present, Cecilia Harker was getting her own way. As she spoke, she masterfully changed subjects without Valerie noticing, almost without effort, and elongated certain words and controlled the lucid pitch of her voice, which made her speech notably more elegant.

Together, they had even started giving weekly hot meals, coal, and clothes to the townspeople. Children were lining the streets with rice and crushed petals in their hands to greet them, young boys were climbing on the thatched roofs to wave and shout their names, and even the merchants would fall silent and stare. Valerie had never been this visible. She felt like a comet that suddenly appeared in the heavens; for her presence presented an imposing and astonishing quality to the crowd, her spectators, alarmed and inspired, stood with mouths agape and eyes widened.

Her resolve to keep away was dissolving. Those early days, she did not know how to move, embarrassingly naive and terrified. She had been wicked, disloyal. These people wanted to love her, waited hours just to see the turn of her head, and Cecilia assured her things would only get better. How could they not when she tried to be worthy of their gaze every day? They were cut from the same cloth. She could not bear to live as she once did, knowing there were days when she did not want to be around, still obscure to herself and this town, crawling for an exit, yet waiting for another blow.

"You don't think they still hate you, do you?" asked Cecilia one day as they, arm in arm, walked back to their carriage. "They adore you, my dear. You have shown them who Mrs. Vertigo is. You're still the mistress here. They are the luckiest lot in the world."

Valerie buried her head in her cloak, trying to hide her smile. Everything resembled a fairytale from that point. Lights twinkled, cheeks turned red with affection. She felt alive under the warm gaze of people; *her* people. Her husband became unusually animated and less ill-tempered, spending his days in his study, devising new plans for spring, mapping new crossroads and festivities to keep the townspeople excited. Labor was a sanctuary in which all found safety, a sort of paradise, fragile yet beaming, simple though it was, where comfort was not a question but something that occurred naturally. Valerie found herself to be one of those happy wives, who granted herself freedom by keeping her husband content, all ghost stories forgotten, and started each day next to her lover.

Ah, Mircalla! She was the only person who was vexed at the sudden arrangement of these precarious affairs, once neglected rightfully, now delightfully tended as one did a garden once the roar of winter expired. Her pretty face became agitated, her manners strange, sulking in her room all day, looking quite heartbroken, and whispering her bitter words of longing, mentioning how wounded she was that Valerie was always away with a flash in her eyes.

"You're always leaving. Away from home, away from me. I close my eyes and picture you, all that I can see is the back of your neck. Long and slender, the tousled curls on your shoulder. I hate looking at your back! I hardly see your face anymore—sockets without eyes, lips no longer mine."

"It's not true, Mircalla. Don't you know that every night I run to your arms? You are my only repose."

Mircalla stood, uncomfortably, shifting from foot to foot, on the far side of her chamber, wrapping her arms around herself. "You abandoned me when your name was written all over my body, when you are everywhere present in me: at the root of my existence. Should I abase myself further? Tear my clothes? Sear my flesh? I will not settle for this, or sigh for a woman who never comes."

"How can you speak so? What can you mean by this?" Valerie asked, crossing the room as she reached out for her. Mircalla sighed and dropped her hand.

"For you, I am but a warped desire."

"Have I failed to show you that I am yours, that I bleed with you when you're wounded? My lips haven't known a tender spirit before yours, my hands have never held one quite as rapturous as you." She exhaled. "Hold my hand."

Mircalla gave a start, then hesitantly pressed her hand. Her eyes were filled with tears.

"There's nothing in this world that will make you untrue. No amount of praise will ever replace your sweet whispers. You loved me as I am. And no matter where I go, in grief and horror, I will always find my way back to you. Always."

Valerie wiped the tears from Mircalla's face. It was surprising how, like a wilted rose, the woman before her melted into nothingness in the blink of her eye. She had shrunk smaller like when she was taken sick; her skin wan and robbed of its luscious glow, cold to the bone, her mouth scornful, her jaw trembling. Yet, it was still her Mircalla Karnstein, who found her in the moonlit garden after she was humiliated, wiping the rolling tears from her flushed cheeks, soothing her worries with the touch of her hand.

"Let's leave the house tonight," Valerie proposed. "I do not wish to see you distraught. Have you eaten today at all?"

"Have you not...noticed?" Mircalla raised a brow, the ghost of a smile lingering on her lips.

"I know." Valerie giggled, her fingers laced at the back of Mircalla's neck, pulling her closer.

"I don't eat human food if I can help it."

"I know."

"I might need to taste you, though. For the sake of our decorum."

Mircalla lowered her head, two rows of sharp teeth flashing, and Valerie threw her head back in anticipation. Instead, Mircalla kissed the spot under her ear then kissed it again. "I want to remember you this way," she said, "in my arms and wild and full of life."

Then her forehead creased with worry more and more with each passing second. Her hand wandered up Valerie's neck, looking for the sharp swell on it, that fading blue, like an old friend. "How's your wound?" she asked, a strand of silver glinting on her back.

Valerie bit her lips. She placed her hand over Mircalla's and felt the bulge, the faint pulse beneath it, a regular pattern that somehow soothed her. The itch was fading from her memory, a sensation not unlike teeth closing around her flesh, ripping a mouthful. A persistent cold, instead, rushing and queasy, was settling between her limbs. The same languid feeling that possessed her lover. Her stomach was sunken and it made her sway like a burst of wind, yet she did not mind the looseness and the latent leap of her intellect and imagination. She had been dreaming the same dreams: Mircalla on her chest, pulsing between the crease of her thighs, streams of euphoria gushing from her mouth with a hunger for more.

Valerie told her that it was almost completely healed, sweating as she spoke, but did not mention any of her dreams.

That night, they sneaked out of Vertigo Peaks again. Valerie peered through the keyhole of her husband's study, and though dim, she could see him pacing around the room, head buried in papers; an empty glass in one hand, a pen in the other, then moved slowly to her room and changed into her runaway clothes—starched chemise, one of her husband's old trousers, and a long coat that clung to the soft curves of her body.

She realized she liked the assortment of clothes and draped layers: a tight corset laced under the chemise, trousers over the knit silk hose for extra warmth. The chilling touch of fabric against her back, the striking contrast of colors. She belonged to two worlds at once, radiant and rounder, slamming and dragging out the momentary and overtired.

Mircalla met her at the back door in the kitchen. Ethel was sleeping on a chair, arm propped under her chin, snoring lightly, and her cap squeezed in her fist. She had a skittish look about her, as though she was waiting for something to break loose, her eyes rolling in their sockets and fluttering the lids in swift motions. A wave of compassion and concern flooded Valerie while Mircalla pressed a finger against her lips and went ahead of her, pushing the door, already ajar, and disappeared into the starless night.

They passed through the woods fleetingly. Their feet did not falter, light and knowing, and soon they were at the clearing again. This time, however, Valerie did not hide in the shadows. She regarded the scene before her on a log, one hand on the side of a pine tree to keep her balance: the crackling of fire before a moment of silence; spotting her vision with ashes scattered to the wind, its dwindling glow reflecting an amber sheen that stung her eyes.

Valerie looked for Mircalla but she had already joined the small group, screaming and twirling around the flames with others; a lurch of bodies, shoving through each other's limp shoulders to get to the essence—another body on the snow. She knew well the sensation that began to soar in the back of her throat. It made such a profound impression upon her mind that she realized escape was impossible. Her teeth were itching, eyes burning, tongue swollen and forcing its way out. It was an act of preservation, she told herself, nothing unlike the hunger for bread and wine.

She approached the scene, staring at the remnants of the body. Her heart was thumping and her hands felt weak. The group's melody was strange to her ears, grating even, and she did not know anyone. There was only the shared thirst that parched their lips, the inhuman cry that almost split their skulls. She retreated a few steps, filled with a desire to go back, unsure of where to look, but then Mircalla appeared beside her, smiling. She did not need any invitations then. She would cross ruined lands and deep oceans if Mircalla held her hand and led the way. There was an entrenched comfort, perhaps a laughable eccentricity for most, woven into her personality that Mircalla ignited. Everything that flamed supposed her presence. Valerie could recite the way her breaths came shallow yet slow, and imagine the gap between her lips that pressed against hers like an ambitious student, for who could stand between this want of hers and this gift? It was all she was made of and Valerie had no desire for another resolution.

They approached the body together, tangled in a sea of crisp arms and bare thighs. A lot of eyes were fixed on her as she was slouching with her head pushed forward, her eyes riveted on the side of the woman's half-eaten face. Her thirst for blood was visceral, exciting, violent; it clawed at her throat and nearly strangled her. She sniffed the woman, circling, treading her feet around the body like a vulture. The smell was sharp but pleasing; a bare, carnal incense that lingered.

She moved her hands, red and numb from the cold, on the uneaten side of the woman's face. It was still warm and with a healthy hue. She would be wise to shut her eyes and sink her teeth, but as her mouth opened, she noticed the red boils on the side of the woman's face, some erupted with scars, some still taut with pus. Her face, contorted and thinned, looked ready to wail. Her silver teeth stuck out, as if to disprove, and Valerie, in horror of recognizing the woman, froze.

It was Lady Catherine. They saw each other two days ago, all tucked in Cecilia's carriage, riding to her cabin by the sea with champagne glasses in hand. They were roaring with laughter, as they were wont to do since the visit to Vertigo Peaks, and bursting into loud chatter, talking about nothing in particular, but having a great time. She was draped in a sage green dress and a hazel-colored muffin on her lap, displaying her luxuriant lashes and rose-tinted lips in the same manner. Lady Catherine whose previous glare had turned into a wary sideways glance. She had not welcomed Valerie with open arms, nor did she expect her to, but she had still left her demeaning attitude aside and engaged Valerie in conversation. But now, juxtaposed against the lingering sensation of friendship, she looked like nothing more than sagging eyes and a lusterless figure.

But the thirst took over. And with tears streaming down her face, Valerie bent over the body, pressing her lips to the horribly pallid and mangled breast, and her throat was bare, showing the two wide punctures which she had not noticed before. The sight of blood splattered over the snow in an enlarging pool, welling up between her teeth and staining her gums like marmalade, made her dizzy. Nothing made a sound except for the blood's squelching on her fingers.

She then danced, nearly overcome with drowsiness and full of blood. Streams of slick, scarlet hands. They fell with a sickening lurch and got up; they came and knotted together like yarn; howling into the thick blanket of woods and snow; finding nothing; falling again; then finding everything.

She too grew fragmentary like a rose bud forgotten among the pages of an old book.

Mircalla pulled her up to her feet, but then the heels of their boots slipped on the blood-soaked snow and they fell, still laughing, on their backs. Suddenly, Valerie thought of her parents whom she'd never met. She was very young when they passed away from another plague, at the age when one's knees were always peeled and hot, and quick thinking led to breathing obsessions. Did she ever want to see them again; one more sweet kiss from their gray lips, a goodbye to mark the passage of time?

She had always had a hole in her chest, longing for the other things, her heart barely true to itself. She wanted to grow less timid, upright like a sapling. Alas! All she ever did was cry in pain. All she ever was a lady on the hills.

She sat up with a sharp pang in her spine and looked at Mircalla. To return as corporeal, she needed her. She needed to taste blood.

"Hold me—tighter—tighter."

Mircalla moved a hand down Valerie's side and nestled her head on her chest, barely breathing. It took a while for her to notice the group's loud cheer thundering across the woods; the thump of their feet on the frozen ground, the wind cutting out syllables and melodies. Burying her face in Mircalla's skin, Valerie noted that there was an odd protrusion, hollow like a cavity, on the edge of her collarbones—two blunt punctures. She felt a ripple of nausea boiling in the pit of her stomach and sprang to her feet, staggering toward darkness, recoiling at the sight of the fire and the corpse and the dancing bodies.

"Where are you going?" Mircalla yelled from behind. A few seconds later, she linked her arm and nudged Valerie to lean her weight on her. She obeyed. "Here, darling. Don't walk fast."

When her feet could no longer carry her, she flung herself to her knees beside a tree, trying not to look back. Mircalla stroked her spine as she heaved and pulled her hair away from her face when her stomach churned and everything left her body—the foamy blood, patches of skin, and all. The midnight mist, stretching far beyond her eye could see, and the acrid smell of acid and the staleness of dirt left her fatigued.

An owl cooed in the distance, the flap of wings slashing through the clump of bellowing voices, and Valerie slid down on the snow. It was as if her heart reached its shimmering fingers into the crust of her skin, tapping at the ribs until they gave way, and the remaining pulp conjured an oscillating motion that crushed her.

Mircalla whispered, "the pain won't last forever." Valerie took a deep breath, the sulfurous fog and wet wood and Mircalla's bitter breath all mixing in her lungs. The night shifted, swimming in one vibrant hue then another, flat and excessive, and Mircalla kept pulling her hair away, her voice all but soundless.

"Are you happy now?" Valerie asked, not trying to hide the resentment in her voice. She had become what Mircalla wanted her to be—a lover, hunter, an erosion hatching in the center of her world. Bent like a twig on a blanket of fresh snow, she regretted many things. Not her bare love for this huntress, but her surrender and the brief moments of not feeling fear. She should have been very afraid when their legs tangled, or her hands slipped under her clothes, or teeth against teeth, tongue against tongue, breaking her into fragments. She needed a life that wasn't just needing her.

"What are you talking about?"

She slowly pulled her knees under her and parted her lips. "Why did you turn me into you? Why did you tear all I had and make me in your image? How can I not hold onto you now?"

This was a confession, yet not the version she thought she'd be uttering. It was a plea to be released, for she had traded one curse for the other. If there was a way out, she did not know where. If she had to stay, she demanded to love and not be good occasionally but everything else was too much to bear.

"Why couldn't you be happy for me? You knew I struggled with my position, that I needed friends to get me through the ebbs and flows of the townspeople's temperament. Why did you lure me here when it is one of those friends that lay lifeless by the fire?"

"Valerie," Mircalla gasped, grabbing her wrist, "They never cared to be your friends. I apologize but I will not bring myself to tears for someone who belittled and derided you, then wore a mask of insincerity. And you were a child addicted to candy, ready to be spoiled by all the mint, fruit, greasy flavor they sell at the stores nowadays!"

Mircalla used her eyes in a provocative, conscious way; her pupils were abnormally large and a glassy film about them made for almost a ghoulish figure. As Valerie writhed slowly on her back near another tree, Mircalla followed. Her lips parted over her white teeth, defiant and insulted by her contempt. In a few moments, her face settled back into its peaceful repose, yet the set discomfort did not desert her eyes.

"Are you really resorting to jealousy to ravage my efforts? Their sneering remarks ran deep, it is true but—"

"This is not jealousy," Mircalla blurted, insolence seeping through her words, and above all, with an air of trepidation. "I'm looking after you. With great love comes a greater responsibility. Isn't this the point of love? To care and look after? They circle around you because you're soaring right now! They will flock to your head and fall upon you without mercy the moment you stumble."

Valerie had come to realize that in looking at Mircalla, she saw only her shudder of vehemence and desperation and the brazen animation in her eyes despite her stiff posture, looking wildly at her face. She approached her with an unwavering sense of defeat, the sinking feeling that was too familiar like when she climbed the stairs to her room as Vertigo Peaks groaned under her feet. Why could not she believe that these women wanted to befriend her and mend their relationship?

"If you will doom me because I love you, then so be it. But I will not tolerate your mistreatments, nor will I stand against your utterly fanciful notions. If you believe you have found your happiness, me tucked in a corner of your house, you sweeping your skirts in the town with women who loathe you, then I am happy for you. But do not ask me to be part of it or watch when it washes you away. I will not be the guest you exchange pleasantries before bed, not anymore. We've passed that point."

"I will not stop you if you don't believe what I say."

In the moment that Mircalla turned away, it seemed to Valerie that she, too, turned. She felt herself standing up and going after her into the dark woods, toward the path they trod, into the familiar world of glistening surfaces. A gust of wind brought the snow down on her shoulders, and Valerie was startled to find that she was still on her knees; that the fire had gone out, and that the singing had stopped.

25

MIRCALLA WAS GONE. HAD it been days or weeks since she disappeared in the woods? The realization of her absence settled upon her slowly, as though it was being awakened from slumber. But once it was before her, tangibly and wide-eyed, it was impossible for Valerie to look away from its translucent body. It followed her with its vacant yet shiny eyes around the house like a listless specter, ever sick and confused by what she was doing, getting heavier with each day. And she, circling around its vicinity, lost sight of herself.

The truth was that Valerie stirred her mind to such fervent inventions because she could no longer defer the blunt pain in her chest anymore. She felt no necessity but to feel; aching with what she wanted to see, to float over Vertigo Peaks' pointed roof, to be carried away on the edge of it, away from everything. Her initial sense of weak optimism had evaporated and Valerie was left with a primal fear and void, unable to tell if she was fixed or moving because Mircalla was no longer there. A landmark of her progress, which moved her from sacrilege to holiness, and she was gone. She felt exposed, passing by faces and places with no recollection.

Still, she kept hearing the news coming from the town. Her husband was crossing from one room to another all day long, his brow furrowed in concentration; sealing one envelope after the other with words wrinkled, ink barely visible from the smudge of his perspiration on paper, and trying to eradicate these attacks that claimed more bodies with an alarming speed. Amidst all that, Cecilia Harker came to visit her almost every day, telling her in detail her preparations for the ball. She had new velvet curtains sewn and had brought eccentric materials for her servants to clean the crystals of her chandeliers. How fast the world was changing! Such advancements would surely be ridiculed a few years ago while everyone was now competing to get their hands on and keep up with the newest trend, wasn't that so?

When she asked Mrs. Harker about Lady Catherine's funeral, the woman's face turned sour and she fixed her eyes on the handkerchief she held in her hand, on which her late friend's initials were delicately embroidered. "It's hard to carry on," she had said, pressing the cloth to her cheek. "I've forgotten how to behave in her absence. It might be hard to believe, but I made sense of the world through her eyes sometimes. A part of me left with her and now I am a little less human."

She had quickly wiped her eyes, took Valerie's hand, and said that the ball must be had. "It's what Catherine would have wanted me to do," she added in a quivering voice, and although Valerie was not sure, she did not object. The next day, when they went to

202

look at their dresses at the tailor's shop, Mrs. Harker was holding a handkerchief with her initials in gold on it.

The Harker mansion seemed to have expanded since her last visit. The rooms were brighter than she remembered. Lights shone from the ajar doors and scattered windows, reflecting the whirl of snow above the sea as the drifts lay deep along the docks. Here and there dried moss projected above it. The snow was falling faster and a dark stream of carriages lined in front of the house; coachmen, butlers, ladies, and gentlemen running in and out of the house, up and down the red velvet carpet laid on the frozen ground. The swell of music and the glimmer of champagne seemed to wipe away the imminent threat of coldness and plague. Valerie, her wrist resting on Ethan's arm, went inside. Vibrant feathers and dark waistcoats; uncertain smiles and open-mouthed conversations; thick breaths and shoulders grazing; the repetitions of orchestra and the bewildering radiance of the many-colored gowns. Everything seemed to be in place—even her. With her iridescent silk taffeta dress trailing behind her, a tepid smile set upon her teeth, and a curious sense of excitement.

However, as they greeted couples and wandered around the hot, sticky rooms, there came upon her a chilling sensation, as though she was under attack, that pulled her muscles tighter and tighter, a sort of indefinable dread that someone was watching her. Her husband was nowhere to be found and Valerie almost succumbed to her nausea.

Cecilia Harker came to her rescue. "Valerie!" She warbled, her voice like an echo in a tunnel, and threw her hands around her. "I am most delighted to see you, my guest of honor! Have you found our small gathering to your liking?"

Valerie shouted over the chatter and music. "Thank you, dear. Very much so."

Cecilia's response was to press her to her side tighter. The lights, the close whiff of perspiration and champagne, the escaping colors—she wanted, for a moment, to sink into one of the chairs to get her breath. "Before I introduce you to the crowd, you must taste the champagne and dance with one of the gentlemen."

"Is that really necessary?" Valerie asked, her head whirling as Cecilia flooded her vision, dragging her from one cluster of guests to another. They finally found a gentleman, a particular Lord Frederick that she had met at Cecilia's dinner party, who reluctantly offered his hand for a dance.

"My Lady Valerie," he bowed, his face expressionless. "May I have the pleasure of this waltz?"

"Of course, Lord Frederick," said Valerie, offering him her gloved hand. As they swept onto the dance floor, the orchestra swelled. She had no special desire to talk; all she demanded was to give herself a chance to doubt the certainty of her past—sickening, treacherous, and without a moment of reprieve. She was not in the least lonely anymore. Nobody questioned her presence. Still, it would not be impossible for anyone to humiliate her. As the final notes of the waltz faded, they came to a standstill, their chests rising and falling with exertion. Valerie's eyes met Lord Frederick's, and even under the glow of chandeliers, Valerie thought he was tainted with the horrible suspicion of that night, never entirely rid of his old nervousness and offensiveness.

As she watched him rejoin the throng, Valerie could not help but feel abashed. He bowed very low to hide his face and stole back hastily to the far side of the room. Had she ever known a place called Vertigo Peaks, a place where apprehension was a skill, and the feeling of not being able to stand anything was as constant as the day's rise—Vertigo Peaks, ah! She fell in love with a woman there once, and now she found it hard to believe it happened at all.

Valerie tried to move but she was in a state of languorous agitation, limp as blades of bright-dew grass underfoot. Voices rose and fell and trembled; beads of sweat dotted the broad foreheads, caressed by the flickering shadow of the guttering candles, and Valerie let these people push her around like a doll, staggering from side to side, drifting from one slick forehead to another, oblivious to the hands that snatch her waist, her necklace, her hair. Then she saw Mircalla. Cecilia knew Mircalla no longer stayed with them at Vertigo Peaks but never once mentioned she was one of her guests. Now, she was dancing with her husband, swirling in the middle of the room as if wading into water; his arm tight on the small of her back, her gloved hand lost in his palm. Whereas Valerie was an intrusive thought, a disturbing arrangement in the room, meddling with everyone else's business, Mircalla and Ethan were darlings of the night, even more so than Cecilia. A sob escaped from her lips. She tried to drown it with champagne but another one ripped her throat, burning within, and she felt the itch throb again. The longer she looked, the firmer she grabbed the glass. They were the only dancers on the floor, twirling in an incessant pool of envy and longing; they cradled the delicious weight of the room in the palm of their hands and all Valerie could do was wriggle with jealousy as the others did.

The music finally stopped and Ethan immediately stepped aside, an agitated look on his face, held together by a frown and beads of sweat rolling down his chin. Mircalla looked around for a long time, an object of envy and desire, showering herself with the furtive eyes and trembling lips. Cecilia emerged by her side, prodding her in the ribs to talk to people.

"This is enough." Valerie put her glass down rather loudly, wiped the streak of champagne trickling down with the back of her glove, and strode to the other side of the room as much as her skirts allowed. A surge of intense frustration, or even something vaguer crept up on her. She did not fight these emotions this time, did not keep herself from feeling them as Mircalla's arched back rose in her vision. There was a phantom truth in them, a twinge of pain and need, demanding too much attention and efforts of will, she knew, but she let them engulf her.

It could have been charming to look at these people. Their delicate movements, improper speeches, or tempting glances might have rekindled what Valerie had long forgotten—that life never went away, drifting by a pendulum, and that it was not hard to enjoy its flow even when one was entirely removed from it. It hurt her to be missing from the scene, more than she anticipated, but in her heart she couldn't find the strength to rejoice and rejoin.

Mircalla fell into the arms of another stranger by the time Valerie edged away from a group of drunk ladies who showered one another with compliments with tears in their eyes. It would have been a heartwarming moment only if one of the ladies did not vomit the entire course of her dinner at Valerie's feet. She retched, feeling hot, and found another corner where she could see Mircalla better. Her husband was nowhere to be found.

It didn't take much time to find her, for she shone among the guests like a mythical creature, sweeping through the room like a raging fire on the horizon, blazing with a color that she had never seen before. She was intense yet sweet to those who danced with her or exchanged looks. Valerie bit her lip, watching the arch of her back spiral around the man's hand like a wisp of smoke, the fleeting image of her ankles as she turned round and round, golden locks of hair barely touching her skin. And there she was headed for refreshments by her partner as the song winded down and the musicians took a break. "Fuck." Her chest rose and fell in shallow surges, pained by this new feeling that cursed her mind like salt on earth. She reeled to one of the tables and got herself another drink. The ice melted on her tongue, the liquor burnt her throat. It felt good. She was lifting up her skirts, swaying from side to side, when Mircalla suddenly appeared by her side.

"What are you doing?" she asked, panting. A ghost of a smile crawled up her lips. She smelled like cigars and wood and Valerie wanted to throw up.

"Drinking." Valerie snorted, tapping on her glass. Mircalla raised a brow. "It has been a while, I presume?"

"No, not at all. This is my first drink actually." Valerie covered her mouth. She hunched over her glass as if to protect it from her view. Mircalla pursed her lips, trying to suppress a laugh. "What are you doing here with us?" Valerie asked. She did not want to say those last words but it was too late; they spilled from her lips before she could catch them. She thought this mythical creature would evaporate any minute. She quivered, an overwrought expression clouding her complexion. Yet, she did not answer. Valerie grabbed her arm, forcing her to look at her face. She thought it would hurt less if she looked at her once more. Nothing could be further from the truth. The room faded. They were two souls wandering on each other's paths. But Valerie needed the truth. "Why did you leave me?"

Mircalla lowered her eyes, staring at her with a great accumulation of terror and despair. She did not speak over a whisper. "I made my demands very clear and you chose to ignore them."

"That's not fair, Mircalla."

Mircalla watched her with a mournful face; she shifted back and forth, concentrating hard, biting her lip. Like a coil tightly wound, she was begging to be released. Valerie was still staring at her stricken face, her glistening eyes, still standing in front of her colossal figure like a helpless child, but a single word ensnared itself in her mind. It was quite disconcerting to feel her power and see how powerless she was. Mircalla breathed hard. Her breath braced her cheeks like a breeze, cold and merciless, as she extended her arm and touched her gently.

"Why did you leave me like everyone else did?" Valerie asked. Her voice sounded strange to her ears and despite the slow music, her heart raced faster. Mircalla held her gaze for a moment then turned around and dragged Valerie to another room. She had gained a new luster as she locked the door, so clear and pure that Valerie forgot her aching for a moment, her hair in the burnished light, radiating that dark and ambivalent valor.

"I cannot live a life unwanted," Mircalla said. Her eyes were cool and she rose taller than before.

"But I want you!" Valerie shrieked.

"This is not wanting. This is an escape for you, a play."

"Come back to me," she replied, but her throat tightened around the words and she felt childish as she spoke. Mircalla smiled.

"Will you dance with me tonight, my dear Valerie?"

Perplexed and her mouth open, Valerie nodded but there was no consolation in this. Mircalla pulled her a little closer, her cheeks flushed, her gaze glinting like ice. Could she hear the flutter of her heart, see the quiver of her lips? She still wanted to press her body to hers, lay her head on the crook of her shoulder, and sway with the sweet music until the end of time, despite knowing it would not last.

"There are many gentlemen in that room who had the honor of holding your hand," Valerie whispered, "of dancing with you."

She looked at their hands, gloved and interlaced together. Their pulse formed a rhythm, a gravity of its own. It hung between them as a separate body, whole in itself, warm.

"Why are we here, then, Miss Karnstein, dancing in this room?"

Mircalla's lips curled in a smile, her teeth bare and sharp. The candlelight glowed on her cheeks, creating shadows under her eyes. Valerie envied her, how she wrapped the entire room around her fingers with an indescribable charm, how even a breeze bent towards the outline of her body.

"Because they are not you, Mrs. Vertigo," Mircalla whispered back. She leaned forward, searching Valerie's face with attention. A single line appeared between her brows, focused and unyielding.

Valerie swallowed hard. Never once had she heard these words, aimed at her, reverberating with such thumping cadence. The voice in the back of her head was crying for answers; she shivered and messed up her steps. Mircalla's laughter rang in her ears. "I would always choose you, whether in a room full of promising men or alone in a lady's house like this. I'd openly insult them all as my arms hung about their arms. Do you know that?"

"No," Valerie admitted. She had an almost irresistible impulse to slide her hand up her bare skin and touch her lips, brace the tip of her finger against the roof of her mouth, see if it quivered like hers, felt like hers, anticipating a move that would rip this room apart and leave them together standing in its ruins, pulse to pulse.

"I've had my fair share of bliss and damnation though it was not always easy to tell which was which," Mircalla breathed in. "However, on that day, when you took me in, opened your home and your heart to me, I knew... I knew I would love you." Mircalla raised her arm and spun Valerie around. She did not hear the music anymore; the sound of her heart palpitating with excitement erased every echo, every melody until every sound rendered itself to a lucid flow. She was on the cusp of revelation, a sight coming from the depths of her soul like a rite and she wanted to dip her fingers to the bottom of it.

"When I look at you, I see who I want to be. I recall, in awe, where I begin. And I end with you. You, you, my darling Valerie."

"Mircalla..."

Valerie gasped. She never wanted to be seen by anyone but her. Now, under her gaze, she roamed and lived and moved like a willow tree. Everything that had been gone from her, all that she had buried in her mind—a feeling of devotion so great that it threatened to engulf her—returned and she let herself be washed in her waves.

Valerie pulled Mircalla in and she kissed her with the hunger she restored day by day in her presence. It was devastating to touch her, consuming every previous desire. Valerie wrapped her arms around her, afraid to let go, and stroked the back of her head. The golden curls were silken in her palms. She held Mircalla down, revealing her neck, and made her way up to her ear with little kisses.

Mircalla moaned and threw her head back, struggling to make room for Valerie as she was already closer than she had ever been before. One of her arms found the indentation on her back and with a little touch, Valerie caved in. Mircalla licked the wound on her neck. The itch returned, coursing through her like an overflowing river. Their hands tangled with the rush, knowing very well that these were stolen moments, calm in the eye of the storm. They had to hurry, put an ease to these bursting flames before anyone walked in.

Mircalla directed them to a tall mirror. She grinned and hugged Valerie from behind, their eyes locked on the mirror, watching their outlines melt into one another, cheek to cheek, hair tangled.

Valerie could notice now the slow and rare beats of Mircalla's heart on her back, as if knocking on her bones to be let in, demanding access. Mircalla moved her hand up from Valerie's stomach to her chest, she stopped right below her breast, feeling the fast pulse on her gloved fingers, responding to the call within. "I already let you in," it was saying, "You are already here, in me, everywhere you can reach for is yours."

"And if it wavers, I will drag and throw it at your feet," Valerie added to the humming inside.

"What a shame we can't keep your heart as it is," Mircalla whispered into her neck, pressing her fingers harder, Valerie pressed a hand on hers. "Take it then," she whispered back, "in whatever form you want it, it is already yours and I will follow you heartless, crawl back to you on my knees wherever you go."

Mircalla kissed her neck.

"This is a very generous offer and I would be delighted to negotiate its terms. But..." She trailed off. Her face darkened, a shiver seemed to possess her. "I'm afraid we must return to the party."

"No, Mircalla—" But nothing else came out of her parted lips. "Come back," she said again, hoping it would convince her. Mircalla kissed her longer with mellow lips then, as if this was the last time.

"I'll come back when you say the truth of your heart out loud."

26

SHE FOUND IT HARD to carry on with conversations, and sat long watching the snowflakes from a window. The night had changed. A sharp stillness had fallen upon the guests, lulled by the sound of wind, and the only thing that was moving at all was a tall figure, casting a long shadow on the deserted drive. The doctor emerged minutes later, standing with his back to the room, and surrounded her in a pensive shade.

"Mrs. Vertigo," he exhaled, brushing snow off his shoulders. He hurried through his words, manifestly ill at ease and keeping a sharp eye about them, and did not wait for her to reply. "I must have a word with you. Immediately."

Valerie did not expect to find him this agitated. His alarm appeared heightened as they passed the dancing couples and servants with empty trays. For a while, he was silent. They were far from the crowd, but not too far to spark rumors. His lumpy hand was slowly twirling the stem of a glass, he turned to her again, and said in the most nervous accents:

"Do you remember the day Miss Karnstein arrived?"

He was out of breath. The familiar steely gaze did not tell her much, yet it was enough to dislike his complexion. She nodded as they walked along the room. Valerie could see the immense heat that hung over the musicians, dancers, host as it dulled their sensibilities with moist and inescapable steam that was gushing from their pores, smearing their faces with an unfriendliness that chilled Valerie to the bone.

"Do you remember the note I meant to give to you?" He pulled out a crumpled piece of paper from his pocket. Valerie nodded again. She tried to speak, to say anything to break the chains of this oppressive moment, but she recalled the man's hardened gaze, the way his seething grip made her skin crawl. He held it between his thumb and middle finger, his pressing gaze still in place, then unfolded it. His knuckles were scarred. Some of the wounds were fresh, uneven marks of bright red. She felt being seized by a sweeping dizziness, a mass of noise and fumes closing around her, when he handed the note to her.

She looked at the paper then at him in the eye, with her blank, unseeing stare, as if she were staring at a gulf and its misty distance. The words spurting from her mouth were crimson as though she was slashed with a sword. "Who gave this to you? When?"

She swallowed and looked at the note again; its yellowed edges, the smudged ink fading in the middle, her half-closed eyes glancing over each curve of the letters. She was fighting against her consciousness, against beginning to see what awaited her.

"Valerie Vertigo is the beast," the note said, "I have proof."

Under the broad strokes of ink, in what was unmistakably her sloping signature, was Cecilia Harker's name. In a panic, Valerie searched the room. Among crystalline, unformed dancers that moved on their own accord and the mellow-toned music, Cecilia Harker was standing. A vague, brittle silhouette, her bright irises rolling one way and the other with the terrible intensity of her laughter. She drew her shoulders together in a moment of re-alization; the plot of all of their conversations, the weariness of all sensations was engulfing her again. She burnt like a ship in a tempest.

As tears welled in her eyes, Mircalla's voice echoed like a bell, unbidden and taunting. She did not hear what the doctor whis-pered in her ear, the voices colliding with another, or protest when Cecilia dragged her back to the crowds. Her host's eyes were hys-terically defiant and remarkable. She was speaking, Valerie could see that, however, not a word reached her ears. She heard her name mentioned before a cheer went up from the buzzing crowd, yet she felt that it was scarcely possible to react. Her body was being dragged on limp legs, the room swimming in and out of focus. In one way or another, her name made all the people, men and women alike, conscious of the same feeling of perturbation, for when Valerie heard her name again, it came with the sound of heels clicking on the polished floorboard. The guests were stepping back; their pale lips parted over the egg-white teeth; brows arched and twitching. Again she saw the same contemptuous expressions, toying with their gloves and ruffles, shoulders slightly raised in a challenging manner.

"My guest of honor," Cecilia was saying, "But many of you know her as the bride of Sir Ethan Vertigo. The mistress of the peaks. But today, you shall meet her again. A side of her, like the new moon, you have never seen before."

Valerie wondered if she had always been thus, like a candle on the verge of guttering, from as far back as she could remember, had she not waited for fate to wreck her, to dissolve into fission, night after night? She did not find it hard to surrender. There was no room for deliverance, she reflected. Cecilia turned on her heels, throwing her hands in the air and spilling a good amount of champagne on the floor meanwhile, then motioned to the other side of the room, into the darkness.

From behind the sea of blurred faces, a silhouette of some-body approached. The lights seemed to follow him. There came a thunder of footfalls, and in the quiet intervals, a low grunting, shattering of glass, shuffling of fans and papers. He was barely more than a shadow, slender and wretched, and although his face was now clean-shaven, and did not have that solemn and unrelenting expression, and his body lithe and graceful, Valerie remembered who this young boy was. She remembered the blazing brightness of Mircalla on him, not knowing then who she was, as she pinned him to the ground with ease and spilled his blood under the glow of his lantern. The stream of crimson against the dying moonlight passing through the icy ground like ripples in the water, the same sense of strangulation that seized his body and left two punctures. He did not meet her eye when Cecilia placed a hand on his shoulder. It promptly gave rise to a wave of gasps and murmurs because talks of decorum, especially when an inferior was involved, restored one's sense of dignity. She had surrounded herself with the need to be noticed and admired, so it became characteristic that the same pleasure occurred to her, especially after her marriage.

And Valerie looked nothing like the image of Valerie that existed before marriage.

"Boy, do you know this woman?" In her drunkenness, Cecilia pushed the tray off the boy's hands and shook her finger. Many in the room held themselves in part discomfort and part disapproval, though their state was as loud and careless. A vein bulged on the boy's forehead as he nodded, his gaze fixed on the floor and shards of glass wet with foam.

"Speak!" Cecilia demanded and dug her nails to his waistcoat.

"Yes, madam."

"How can someone like you know an esteemed lady like Mrs. Vertigo? Answer immediately."

"I—" The boy raised his head, looking directly at her. Valerie was accustomed to looks of perpetual exasperation, eyes grappling with disgust and awe at the same time. Yet, she had never been held under a gaze so rancorous and merciless that she couldn't breathe. He did not make the least effort to conceal his insolence.

"I saw the lady in the woods, madam. She attacked me."

Whispers turned into screams. They were mouthing the words over and over again like rings of sand in a desert, grating and sweltering, and their brows were slick with sweat. Valerie did not feel a thing for herself, but only the crack of her wrists as the crowd whirred in anticipation. She closed her eyes and listened to the inciting sound and cutting terms. They were considerably excited. She was no different from her surroundings. Only then she opened her eyes again.

Behind Cecilia, the boy shifted slightly, flashing a glance at the crowd who weighed him up and down, left and right. And Valerie noticed how bony his fists were, half of his face hidden behind the flimsy fabric of his suit, idly turning on his heels, nodding vaguely as his mistress spoke.

"Poor Felix—my poor, lovely Felix. He has never quite healed." She tilted her head and quavered toward the end, as though she was coming loose. Rose-gummed, vindictive, unforgiving. In one swift motion, Cecilia reached for his throat, curled her fingers around his chalky necktie and ripped it free. It slithered to the floor.

"Tell them what she did to you." Cecilia was circling around him, brushing her fingers around his waistcoat and shirt.

"This lady and her friend assaulted me in the woods. I saw them pressed against a tree... unladylike... intimate. There was blood and

I called out to them, not knowing who they were, and demanded what they were doing. I don't remember much more but I toppled backwards, the shadow—her friend—charged across the hollow, dove straight at me, and two needles pierced my neck. Miss Mircalla Karnstein she was, her friend."

27

FOR A SUSPENDED MOMENT, nothing happened. Then Cecilia ripped the boy's buttons, sent them scattering them across the room, and revealed his neck. The marks rose higher and higher, to his chin, then almost to his ears. Every inch of his skin was covered in sanguine and violet, as though painted by a rough hand, deep veined and wrinkled like an old man. But there was the discolored and bulging wound right before her eyes. It was straining against the naked whiteness of his own skin, throbbing and opaque in appearance. He pressed a hand over it, feeling its gnarly shape, then with eyes protruding from their sockets, returned Valerie's gaze.

"This adulterous woman is the root of our misery! She has been infesting our town with sickness and famine. And we may never see the light, and lest we intervene, she will cling to the bottom of our world and suck the life out of it!"

She searched the room hopelessly. Cecilia knocked her down with a swat of her hand. She was indignant. Flaming waves of humiliation rose from Valerie's chest when she saw Ethan. He was standing under the staircase, stooping forward, as if he were physically hurt, and peering with wide eyes at her. His lusterless gaze swept from the boy's neck, down his bare chest and to her struggling to her feet. But he did not move, only scratched the tip of his black mustache.

A faint breath fanned the back of her neck and the chilling sensation spread to chest. Someone took her arm and drew her up. The word came out so choked that nobody moved. "Mircalla."

Valerie fought to breathe, the sting of her shame coiling around her like barbed wire, until Mircalla lowered her head, folding the smooth skin, and looked at her. It was a moment of freedom, no matter how fleeting it was, until a gleam of light fell on her lap. She seemed to be filled with warmth, streaking through her mind as if she were on a precipice, but then Cecilia howled and slashed the boy's neck. The wound burst open like an arch of carnations. Turning her head, Valerie could see the flesh tearing, his shirt crusting in red-brown stains. The boy whined, staggering and swaying.

"They feed on our blood and betray our flesh! Look! Look at how their teeth press against the lips. Do you hear the sounds deep from their throats, through their noses?" Cecilia pushed the boy aside and stomped her feet.

The view induced a feeling Valerie had become so familiar over the course of months, inspired not by the gravity's pull but by the infinite reaches of her hunger. She almost fell, lurching over the broken glass and sticky champagne; sweat broke out on her skin.

It was the sight of blood that made her thus feral, climbing up her groin, the flat of her hands, to her temples. Valerie clenched her muscles against the feeling, but it only lasted for moments, and then she sprang on the boy. But before she could sink her teeth into his chest, Mircalla pulled her back. The boy yelped and sprinted back to the staircase.

"Bestial, degenerate, foul! That's what this family is. Damned be Ethan Vertigo and his schemes for wreaking havoc on us! He has poisoned our lives from the day his sister went missing to the day he took her as wife."

What a white, blue-veined face that was! "You deceived us... Your purity was a hoax... We prayed for an heir... You're rotten... Shame on you! Give us back our grace! Shame on you! Look us in the face! Shame on you! You've taken our hopes! Shame on you! Shame! Shame!"

Valerie took notice of Cecilia's wrinkles about the eyes, the lips that bared a dazzling set of teeth, her chin stiff with tension that drew her back. She was wildly looking at people every now and then to see whether they were listening. She possessed the place and walked confidently to her, wheezing merrily under her breath, as she passed her and stood before Mircalla.

It happened in the blink of an eye. Mircalla's wind whipped around her, cold and ravenous as she pulled the body. She snatched Cecilia Harker with the flick of her wrist and lifted her, turning her around, then bit at her throat, hard, and at the same moment, blood seeped onto her tongue, trickling down her chin. Cecilia could not even open her mouth before she jerked to a stop turned stiff as a board. A coat of wet blood on the pristine satin of her gown, glistening under the chandeliers, and Mircalla did not let go of Cecilia, letting the bystanders stand in terror, easing the curve of her back in pleasure.

"Spare us," the crowd begged and Valerie noticed that they were huddled in a corner, sagging and sour-smelling, covered in a fine layer of sweat and blood. Mircalla must have pierced both arteries to splatter them thus, she thought. A vibrating feeling warmed her hands, then nestled on the burning itch that kept her awake night after night. Nothing was too much trouble for her anymore. As the house held its breath, she crawled to the twisted silhouettes of Mircalla and Cecilia, pulsing with urge. She wanted blood. She needed every drop to sweep her veins, claim the untouched parts of her body. Slick, irresistible, delicious, and copious.

"Come closer. Look at this." Mircalla smeared warm blood on Valerie's sleeves and wrapped an arm around her. The bewildered sparkle in her gaze had expanded, as if to hold Valerie within.

Her eyes opened, unseeing, misty, and swimming in a languor of desire. It was her husband, yelling at her face, forcing her to her feet; his face distorted with a kind of torture that sickened Valerie. She shoved him aside. A sea of people carried him away quickly.

Valerie's aching legs gave way, and she almost fell to her side. Mircalla cupped her face. She trickled a crimson line down her cheeks, on her neck, and she began to pulsate with anticipation. A life such as this needed no elucidating; she could grab and pluck it from its roots and make it her own. She would evade the withstanding solitude, pacing in the darkened rooms of Vertigo Peaks—afraid of the faces that followed and crept behind her window no more, and make them all prey to feast upon—and months of rancor would vanish in this room if she wanted. Her heart raced faster; her breaths were sharp and shallow. The air was not enough to fill her lungs; the fuel was somewhere else, Valerie knew.

Mircalla stroked her hand and put it over the open wound. Deep cuts on the flesh, punctures and shining bones.

"Be willing, heart of mine," she whispered as Mircalla ran a finger on her lips, tracing the edges with a taste of her future. A vampire she was to become. She bared her teeth in a feral snarl and sucked on the skin. A gush of blood washed her face as she pinned Cecilia with the back of her hand. She licked the wound and lingered on the jagged edges, searching for all the stolen moments in her life. The longings of her heart, the murderous threshold that twisted her stomach and grew inside her like an uprooted tree.

A sharp pang surged within her. The pain of finally giving in after refusing what had been brewing in her heart for a long time. Ever since she met Mircalla, necessity became trifling. It was another burden pulling her down like a tidal wave, keeping her afar from the shore.

What she swore to protect came back to taunt her in violent ways; the Vertigo legacy turned out to be smoke and brittle bones nestled in the arms of a cursed, indifferent husband.

Who could blame her if she willed herself into another existence? Who could dare to question the flare of her anger against this town and its people—who, in the naked glory of her husband, consumed her very being and tossed it aside, spewing out curses and gossip?

"Feel it," Mircalla instructed, patting her back and whispering in her ear with a wide grin that gleamed on the pointed edges of her teeth. "Does it not feel good? Filling yourself with pleasures unspoken and undreamed of? You waited and waited. Fatally wounded inside, chained to the same man that rejected you, aiding and abetting others to harass you. But I'm here now and all your lusts shall be named and satiated, if you want so."

She planted a kiss on Valerie's forehead. Heat rose to Valerie's cheeks as Mircalla's chest crushed against hers and Valerie was surprised she didn't crumble into pieces.

It took some time for her to understand, as Mircalla pushed a lock of hair from her face, that she would lapse into agony and die an awful death, no matter how it may strike, because Mircalla was the life-blood, not promised but earned with toil, that turned her thoughts and courage rapaciously to herself—cruelly flung into the jaws of oblivion, for such confines Vertigo Peaks vindicated—that, in spite of the stirring malice of those blood-thirsty townspeople, she was still tender at heart. For her—the exquisite Mircalla Karnstein.

"I love you," Valerie said.

28

MIRCALLA'S FLIGHT WAS DECLARED an indication of her crimes and the screams in the frigid air found their way back to her. Valerie had little to protect herself from the stinging gusts of wind as she was carried away by a throng of hands that towered over her. They were shredding her gown, spitting on her face. Red with Cecilia's blood her hands shone for a moment, and then she laid on the snow in the moonlight.

She was full of blood. Its undulating waves wrapped around her limbs, layered and deep, like the twisted roots of a tree. She felt weightless, bearing the nature of an apparition under the mist of the peaks like a prize: superlatively powerful and full of love. Valerie did not know what spell Mircalla cast upon the room, limbs frozen in horror, unable to move or scream, but she was grateful. Even if she wouldn't see her again, she was grateful.

When she arrived at Vertigo Peaks hours later, it was just before dawn. The wind had turned and the world was broken. The sounds of drums and lips moving and breaths grumbling floated in the air, which blotted her memory. She found herself walking in a circle with the distraught Vertigo Peaks at its center, its dark stones and warped wooden floors barely hidden from view as the edge, the curl of flames shimmered off the walls and bathed the dawn in a deep radiance.

"Run! Save your life!" It was the doctor stumbling out of the manor-house, a leather-bound tome in hand, choking back a cough. Pillars of flame licked at the day's earlier sunlight, casting grotesque shadows that danced on the stricken physician's face. Valerie glimpsed remnants of a familiar warmth but did not dwell on it. Another blast showered pieces of paned windows; a lone sentinel pointing to the billowing smoke. The doctor disappeared without another word, plunging back into the searing maw of the house.

Valerie heard his boots crunching on fallen plaster, his gloved hand brushing soot-blackened portraits lined like persecutors on the wall. She had relied on her hearing no more than a schoolgirl, but this was the first time her delicate ears commanded the violent scene before her, alert as wild creatures slithering through grass.

She found her husband on his knees under the window of his study. The heat was oppressive here, the air thick with the cloying scent of burning wood and singed flesh. Her eyes were stinging with tears and she saw his legs bent in a strange way through a cloud of smoke. The glow of his hands isolated a skull in all its jagged lines and corners, more shadow than a substance, between his burnt frilled collars. He blew a low, painful moan, like a lamenting song, and banging his head on the bone. She found a half-written letter by his side, the ink smudged by tears, addressed to him from Emery Vertigo. It was the letter that Valerie had taken from his study and forgotten about. It laid there like a cracked crucible of their marriage.

He turned his glassy, unseeing eyes to her when she touched the skull, as if in a dream. Valerie watched the patch of light flit across his face like a magpie. Behind the hollow of the bleached skull, the face of her husband flamed, as he crumpled the hems of her skirt in his fists.

"What have you done?" She asked in disgust. The man was lying on his back, rigid and writhing like a worm, staring up at the skull.

"I can't take this pain any longer! Here—here, take her! I can't stand it! Yes! Yes, I killed her. I have nothing left to give! You fool! She burns my heart—Ah! Father, do not forsake me. I did what you asked!"

Valerie wished he would stop. There was a strange sound in her ears like heels dancing on floorboards. Louder it became, louder and enthralling. Meanwhile, Vertigo Peaks throbbed; a single, on-going groan; its sharp roof teetering on the edge of collapse. And Ethan was still talking. Faster and faster, as if possessed by the spirit of his dead sister.

"I loved her! The house—my father—warned me. It claims me. The curse repeats itself. Look! Look at me. I'm falling apart—Hold it, do not let it go! My father wants the house—I want my sister—I love her." He picked himself off the frozen ground, waving the paper before her eyes. "He said it would be me—the legacy, the bloodline. Dog-hearted fiend! Ah, let me be mad! Where has he been but inside me? He held my hands. No blood was shed. Strangled into silence. But why does it not stop? I did what he asked!"

He floundered through the deep snow, beating the sides of his head with his fists and weeping uncontrollably.

"For God's sake, end his misery!"

The doctor collapsed next to his friend, gasping for breath as the salvaged artifacts scattered around him as the manor's roof caved in with a thunderous boom, and cradled his friend to his chest, tears streaming down his soot-streaked face. "Put an end to his misery," he repeated, rubbing his hand gently on her husband's forehead, his voice cracking. He was in despair. There was something haunted about it; a kind of strange and resigned peace. Valerie had come to realize how needed this language was—increasingly fearful of the same death that awaited them. She knew she would kill them. The doctor knew that too. It was by no means easy, but it was not terrible either.

"Why?" she asked. Something was weakening within her. She was not sure why she asked the question. She did not know if she cared for an answer, either. Perhaps, it had happened all her life, this waiting for an answer, of being sealed by wonder. A slate of radiance had fallen on their hands, their twisted bodies, around their heads, too bright and ominous for early morning.

"He won't live much longer anyway. Vertigo Peaks is no more, and Ethan will be dust with it. Everybody knows. You were the final sacrifice."

She lowered her gaze, and a sharp chill settled deep between her bones. She saw it now: the prayers, legs curled and tears soaking through the sheet. The townspeople were on their knees for the house. They wanted an heir so she could wither and perish by her husband's hand. It was foolish of her to dream of dull days and dreamless nights, to make it through the year and avoid longing.

The hollows of her feet were aching. When the doctor held Ethan in his arms, Valerie could see the top of his head, the dark tumble of his hair. The dark breadth of him beneath the licking flames was wintry—drab and bare. They were holding each other close in the growing dawn, Vertigo Peaks burnt, the footfall of the townspeople rumbling thunderously. What was left that could hold her back? A voice in the distance said something, she could not make it out, and the surrounding hollows echoed with cries.

Only then did she notice the glint of the scalpel. The blade was clean, a tarnished silver, and she snatched it without thinking. She did not ask herself what she could do; the question was inconsequential. She looked at her husband's blood-red eyes, the luminous purple of dawn flickering on the deep furrow between his brows. She should remember the soft melody of birds, overwhelmed by the approaching steps of the townspeople, yet still beautiful. The back of her knee scraped on the stone walls of the house, and murmurs of Mircalla floated in her ear. Mircalla. She was permanent, coming upon her with no whispers of what she had not done. Mircalla. She would sit there and wait for hours to be called by her. To be wanted by her.

She could see herself now, timid beyond measure, stealthy in her evening dress, desperate and filled with an intense desire to fill a place that was never emptied, to please. It came too late for her, the confidence and righteousness of her love.

She turned the steel handle of the scalpel in the flat palm of her hand, pressing the metal hard. She was about to drag her husband by the hair to a secluded corner, but changed her mind, her hand in midair, and pulled the doctor's hair instead. The sight of him brought back the feel of anger and resentment—or more importantly, vengeance—as she plunged the scalpel on his tongue, again and again and again. He stirred and turned his head, but did not block the blade. A trickle of warm blood slowly ran down, making a small puddle at her feet, soaking her hands. He was still holding Ethan, hanging over him like a bird of prey, nearly suffocating him. She was violently pulling on his tongue, inserting the scalpel into his mouth, and it eventually was ripped from its base. The blood seeped, then shined, then spilled from the edges of her husband's face and a low murmur buzzed through the wind.

"This is the last you'll see of him. Your lips won't form his name, for your tongue speaks double, and it simply cannot be trusted. You're unworthy of your flesh. Maybe, now that your tongue has taken a new shape, it won't betray anymore, be deceitful. Maybe, just for once, you will be able to speak my language," Valerie said, shoving the speechless man aside, "Now watch."

Valerie was surprised to see how powerful her hands were, carrying the scalpel so well. The sky was soft and blue, free of the mist and smoke from the chimneys. She closed the distance between her and her husband, looking down at his ghastly figure. He was still holding the skull, as if his sister was hiding in its hollow sockets. He looked too soft, too vulnerable to be a killer, but that was his thing: His disarming smile blended well with the erratic and fierce movements of the townspeople. Deadly when he wanted to be. He perhaps never got on with his father's commands, but he had to struggle for the legacy he left behind and promised him. He sure learned the sweeping mobility of his people's favors, and showed no signs of blame. Perhaps that was what drove him to her: her callous disdain for the masses, sometimes needing the drowsy hum of his voice, trusting him with his longing for some greater change in the people.

"I relied on your charity, you know?" she said, hovering over his head. "I never mistook it for love. But with a grateful heart, I came here. Now, look at what you've made me. This is your design, your lesson, your curse. I would learn to be better and give you all my strength if you hadn't betrayed me, so save your tears, husband. Vengeance will serve me better."

Now people were at the gates, calling her to come out, grinning with satisfaction, for they knew she would never repent or confess. She did not find in her heart to mend anything. First, they made her a saint, then a traitor. Finally, Mircalla made her a lover. Everything that passed did so without any impression upon her. She was Valerie Vertigo no more.

A heavy grating sound revealed the iron gates being forced open. The hands clinging to the rusted bars were free and they were coming straight to her. This was not the aimless crowd she watched day after day, lusterless and smoldering, but they walked briskly to the manor-house. The group dispersed momentarily before merging together. There were two new figures at the front, hollow-cheeked and solitary, following Valerie with a sunken expression. The white-hot sun cast a dejected glow on their thinned faces. By instinct, Valerie touched the puncture marks on her neck, throbbing and itching. They were frothing at the mouth, the whites of their eyes dark and moody. Ethan was saying something but the crowd's roar drowned him out. She noticed the doctor crawling towards the edge of the forest from the corner of her eye.

"You are lost forever," he said over and over again, tears running down his cheeks. He was bright and spotless under the sun, wailing in anguish, inhumanly piercing, as he threw himself to his side. His suffering was a prompting she had been waiting for. She was consumed by an unquenchable rage and aversion, the depths of which she no longer tried to disguise.

She folded her arms around his chest, elbows poking through his ribs, unraveling the threads of his mortal flesh. There was the heart; there laid what she was seeking. She lowered her arm and swung the blade, slamming it into his chest, directly against the hollow where his heart was. She thought life was too short to be spent in animosity when death was just as good a medium. It did no good for her to condemn these hapless men, spectators of her doom, or laugh at them. She had to seek more, and she finally did.

There was screaming and the sound of bone crushing. Her soul demanded labor, so she struck again and again. His blood was thumping in the hollows of her palms. Valerie was seized by such vitality that was shaking her body that it extended beyond the limits of her skin. She remembered that love was wild—the earth immense—and she was capable of receiving them both in an embrace with an untiring hope.

Blood painted a bright halo around him. Valerie witnessed his tremors and convulsions growing sparse, and heard the bursts of air escaping from his lips before he died. He seemed to disappear under her weight and only the skull pressed to his cheek remained, reverberating against the soft crease of her thighs. She breathed a sigh of relief as if a great weight was off her chest and fell on her back.

29

SHE HAD BEEN IN such a haste for all these months, lulled by the sound of cheers and the chilling air, but now, she had a sense of relief and retrospection, as though she had at last stood up from her shadowed corner and faced the daylight. She feared she might die, the heavy languor soaking her, passing the terrors of disease deeper. She had long felt like a piece of meat at a butcher's shop, unrolled and put on display, ready to be carved and sold. Her limbs and hands were lead heavy and she was aware of a stupor of immeasurable exhaustion; it was, perhaps, the first time she had time to consider herself: weary, thirsty, yet alive.

Someone blocked the sun and Valerie cracked one eye open. A few extended arms, reaching for her, crept closer to her face. A tremor ran along her as familiar fingers caressed her cheek. "Mircalla," she moaned, throwing her head back. The townspeople were wandering in circles, dazed and blind, like a flock of birds that lost direction. The vastness of the hills and swirling veils of clouds over the peaks mesmerized her; to be encircled by the gentle pattern of their overbearing presence was soothing as each with their own personality, their unpeopled totality, the quality of reaching nowhere produced within her a sense of intimacy.

"Get up, darling."

Her dear Mircalla. Voracious and terribly relentless. She came back to her. Something within her told her that she was going to survive no matter what.

"Are you really here? Speak, Mircalla."

Mircalla did not rush. She pulled Valerie to her feet and pressed her to her chest. Valerie wanted to describe the loneliness back to her, and bridge the days spent in her absence, but all she could do was fill her lungs with the musky smell of hers, a mixture of smoke and earth and sap. Valerie thought about the tormenting nights she spent in Mircalla's room, pressing her palms against the moonlit windows, hoping to catch a glimpse of her billowing cape or cascading hair. The warmth of her lips still grazed Valerie's cheeks even then; moments of passion and sincerity wrapped her like a warm blanket. Hours spent in sweet conversation and tenderness, trust and security were all gone, and days were drained of reason, nights became bottomless with misery. She tossed and turned like a sleepless child, waiting and waiting.

She lost everything because she could not face the truth until it was too late.

"I ruined it all. My lapse of judgment, forgetting I was once their enemy made every error more malignant than it ought to be. I blamed you, exploited your benediction, left you in fear and perplexity. It was a cowardly thing, more than enough to send you away indeed, to accuse you for unchanging and not extending the grace for my so-called friends. How will I ever live, knowing all bonds of familiarity are eradicated from your heart and rightfully so? I'm bleeding—bleeding inside! I had not intended to rise in mutiny against you, the lips that fed me. What will be my worth? Tell me, Mircalla."

Under the sun, Mircalla's skin had a blue tinge, a waxy formation like the back of a newborn's ear. Her lips were parched. All power seemed to have drained from her, the whites of her eyes showing, yet she moved her mouth into a smile, though it lasted for a moment.

"Valerie. My dearest Valerie, look!"

Mircalla was extending her fingers over the drive where the townspeople paused their obstinate circumambulation. Some were kneeling in front of another group and clasping their hands, as though greeting great heroes; others were poised on their toes, arms limp by their sides, like birds about to take flight. In Mircalla's quietness, Valerie gathered her thoughts. She felt impelled to move towards the crowd to ease the feeling in her chest but Mircalla held her back. Without the shelter of Vertigo Peaks, she no longer felt the eyes following her with indifference.

"You'll meet them later," she said. "Stay here with me now."

"Who are they?"

"You know who they are. You met them in the forest."

Valerie sucked in a sharp breath. They were silent again: Mircalla, somber, Valerie incredulous and fairly strained. The deeper gust of recognition flashed before her eyes. She remembered the dancing, the howling, faces melting into one another, teeth sharp and wanting.

"Are they like you? Vampires?"

Mircalla gave her an awkward nod, almost curt, and Valerie felt her weight fall dead on her, stealing away her breath.

"We won't be alone anymore. We won't churn on our bellies for companionship, my love. They found us. We will leave this abomination of a land behind and write our destiny, root ourselves wherever we want. However," she paused, suddenly breathless, trembling. "The blood in your veins does not belong to you anymore," Mircalla began, squeezing her hand. "The transformation had already begun, my venom courses in your veins. I bit you when you still had time. Before the curse ate you alive. I wouldn't have liked to steal the life you deserve if I had the choice: prosperous and joyful and undecided. I would not have rendered you a beast, a deviation, like me. But I did not have a choice, my dear Valerie. I could not lose you."

She took her hand and raised it to her lips, softly kissing between her knuckles. "Don't take my bitterness as yours although I am mad at you." She sighed. "I am mostly angry at myself for not stepping in sooner."

Cold tears trickled down Mircalla's cheeks and landed on her shoulder like rain. Valerie cupped her chin, almost choked on her words, realizing she was on the verge of tears too. "You made me in your image. You carved me and breathed me into life. Where you ache, I tremble in agony. I never had to see where I stood because I was with you, hand in hand, heart against heart, and I am replenished by the same thing that brought you to me."

Valerie gestured to the blood stains creeping up her arms. "Because my heart sought the same. I do not regret anything, I am not ashamed. Killing was an option and I had chosen wisely. I took what was mine. The rest...they did this to themselves."

She thought of the times she was ravished with blood, captured by something vital and undeniable, her teeth aching to stir and open wounds. The act was so freeing, so rapturous even, that she did not think it was prompted by a venom nearing her heart. It had always been a part of her, maybe long before she met Mircalla, but it was Mircalla who saved her when no one else did.

"When?" she asked. Words were eluding her throat.

Mircalla took on a haunted look, watching the group approaching. Her teary eyes were larger than she had ever seen before. Yet, surprisingly, nothing in them was fearful.

"I don't know," she admitted. "Living during the day will be like daydreaming: a prolonged unconsciousness rooted in and cured by wandering, glimpsing at the horizon and waiting for the dark veil of the night to fall. You will be fragile in those hours, hanging between collapse and exhaustion, but the night will heal you.

There came a pause, then Mircalla turned to meet her gaze, and to Valerie's amazement, her eyes were misty again. "You will rid yourself of your human blood too. The venom will replenish the cold, insatiable vampire blood minute by minute. You'll wake up stronger; you will wake up anew," she said and laced their fingers together. The words were elongated and changed, and there was something cruel about them that made Valerie's heart jump. "You will have no recognition of yourself. Hunger you will become, a hunger that leads nowhere but blank ferocity. You will not remember who you were at all."

Valerie jerked. She wanted to free herself from her embrace, the lulling whisper of her voice. She could not lose Mircalla once again when she only found her.

"Will I remember you?" she asked, breathless, now gripping her lover's arms so tightly her knuckles first reddened, then went white.

Mircalla's cheeks glistened with tears. She shivered as Mircalla tucked her into an embrace and she came to rest on her chest.

"No," she said. Then quickly added, "Not at first." A ghost of a smile played on her lips. "But I will come back to you in a dream. I will bear my name with the wind, wail like a newborn baby, until you hear it and turn to it. I will whisper it to trees and mountains and lakes and maidens until one day, you remember me. A storm ravaging your house, a mark on your neck, a body in your bed. Then, we will meet again."

She held her hands and kissed the blood-soaked tips. One by one.

"I am afraid," Valerie whispered, picking at her lips. "I don't have the strength in me to let you go. I can't control it. How will I let you go, Mircalla? How will I be?"

"We will be okay. I will hold you close every day until you remember."

"Promise me."

Valerie pressed her lips against hers, locking herself in the fleeting moment before everything was lost.

"I promise. Do not be afraid."

Valerie looked at her with a furrow, unsure of the direction they would take. The moment had passed, and the deed was done. She smeared her hands on the snow; her husband's blood stared back at her, luminous and sinister. She had pierced the Vertigo Peaks through its heart and now it was bleeding, where it belonged until it drained all their history.

The group was waiting for them by the greenhouse. Valerie pushed a stray hair away from her face and smiled. Perhaps, she thought, she could be someone new. Mircalla kissed the top of her head when she spoke. "Know this, Mircalla. In all my memories, you burn the brightest. You painted a whole new sky and set it on fire so we could see the world ablaze. If not for everything, this alone is enough for me. I'll always crawl my way back to you."

For the first time in her life, she could choose to leave. The words were light as a feather on her tongue, rolling against the roof of her mouth as sweet as cream. Soon, she would carry another heart, unfamiliar to her, yet dearer than anything she had known.

Then, they, hand in hand with wandering steps, through the peaks took their way.

Acknowledgements

For me, *Vertigo Peaks* was a work of acceptance as much as of love. I would not have dreamt about writing this book or dug deeper with these characters if I had not decided to leave so many things behind in the last couple years. And I certainly would never be this proud if it weren't for my family, my friends, and my cat. I hope whoever reads this book is reminded of someone they would find and fall in love with in thousand iterations, even when they know they can't go back.

Thank you. I love you. I'm still here.

To stay connected with Dion, visit her website on dionanja. wordpress.com or follow her on Instagram (dionwrites), TikTok (authordionanja), Twitter (thedionyrtal), and Tumblr (dionyrtal).

About the Author

Dion Anja is a poet, author, and a lover of all things uncanny. Weaving grotesque and ravishing characters into her writing, she hopes to lure you into the chilling landscapes of her stories. When she is not writing or reading, Dion can be found cuddling with her cat or taking long walks in the forest.

Also By Dion

Poetry

My Dawn Is Only Five Hours Away (2020)
Motion Sickness (2022)

Made in the USA
Middletown, DE
13 March 2024

51360413R00149